ᵀʰᵉ FINEST HOURS

THE FINEST HOURS

THE TRUE STORY OF A HEROIC SEA RESCUE

MICHAEL J. TOUGIAS & CASEY SHERMAN

SQUARE FISH

Henry Holt and Company

NEW YORK

SQUARE
FISH

An Imprint of Macmillan
175 Fifth Avenue
New York, NY 10010
mackids.com

Our books may be purchased in bulk for promotional, educational, or
business use. Please contact your local bookseller or the Macmillan Corporate
and Premium Sales Department at (800) 221-7945 ext. 5442 or by e-mail at
MacmillanSpecialMarkets@macmillan.com.

Library of Congress Cataloging-in-Publication Data available

ISBN 978-1-250-04423-5 (paperback)   ISBN 978-0-8050-9765-8 (ebook)

Originally published in the United States by Henry Holt
and Company, LLC / Christy Ottaviano Books
First Square Fish Edition: 2015
Book designed by Ashley Halsey
Square Fish logo designed by Filomena Tuosto

10

AR: 6.0 / LEXILE: 1140L

*To the heroes, those they saved
and those who never made it back to shore,
and to Adam Gamble, a real Cape Codder*

—M. J. T. & C. S.

THE FINEST HOURS

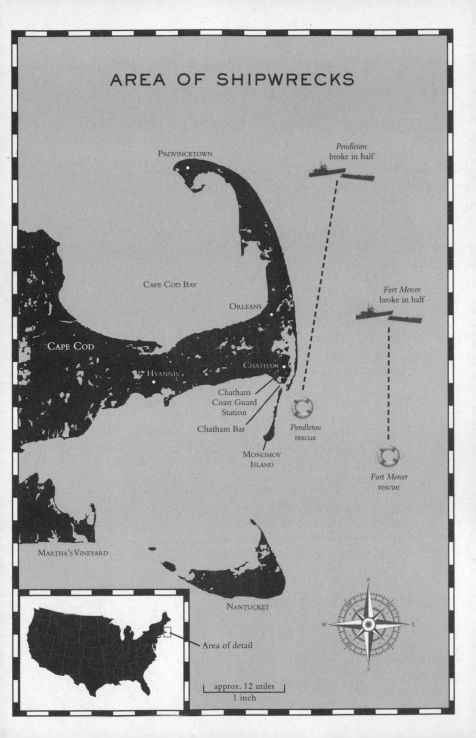

AREA OF SHIPWRECKS

Pendleton
broke in half

PROVINCETOWN

CAPE COD BAY

ORLEANS

Fort Mercer
broke in half

CAPE COD

CHATHAM

HYANNIS

Chatham
Coast Guard
Station

Chatham Bar

Pendleton
rescue

MONOMOY
ISLAND

Fort Mercer
rescue

MARTHA'S VINEYARD

NANTUCKET

Area of detail

N

W   E

S

approx. 12 miles
1 inch

CONTENTS

PART III

INTRODUCTION

SHIPS, CAPTAINS, CREW, AND RESCUERS

On February 18, 1952, an astonishing maritime event began when a ferocious nor'easter split in half a 500-foot-long T2 oil tanker, the *Pendleton*, approximately one mile off the coast of Cape Cod, Massachusetts. Incredibly, just 20 miles away, a second oil tanker, the *Fort Mercer*, also split in half. On both fractured tankers, men were trapped on the severed bows and sterns, and all four sections were sinking in 40-foot seas. Thus began a life-and-death drama of survival, heroism, and a series of tragic mistakes. Of the 84 seamen aboard the tankers, 70 would be rescued, and 14 would lose their lives.

Here is a list of the men involved with each part of the tanker sections who are discussed in the book:

PENDLETON
RESCUE

Pendleton Stern
Raymond Sybert, chief engineer
Charles Bridges, seaman
Frank Fauteux, fireman
David Brown, first assistant
  engineer
Henry Anderson, "wiper"
  maintenance worker
Fred Brown, second "wiper"
Wallace Quirey, third assistant
  engineer
Carroll Kilgore, crewmember
George "Tiny" Myers, oiler
Rollo Kennison, crewmember
Aaron Posvell
Aquinol Oliviera, cook
Oliver Gendron, seaman

Rescuers on the *CG 36500*
Bernie Webber, captain
Richard Livesey, seaman
Andy "Fitz" Fitzgerald, engineer
Ervin Maske, crewmember

Chatham Station
Daniel W. Cluff, station
  commander
"Chick" Chase, boatswain's mate
Mel Gouthro, engineman first class

Pendleton Bow
John J. Fitzgerald Jr., captain
Herman G. Gatlin, seaman

Rescuers on a 36-foot motor lifeboat
Donald Bangs, chief
Emory Haynes, engineer
Antonio Ballerini, boatswain's
  mate
Richard Ciccone, seaman

FORT MERCER
RESCUE

Fort Mercer Bow
Frederick Paetzel, captain
John O'Reilly, radio operator
Jerome Higgins, crewman
Edward Turner, purser
Vincent Guldin, third mate
Willard Fahrner, first mate

Rescuers on the Cutter *Yakutat*
J. W. Naab, captain
Gil Carmichael, crewman
William Kiely, ensign
Paul Black
Edward Mason Jr.
Walter Terwilliger
Wayne Higgins
Bill Bleakley, communications officer
Dennis Perry
Herman Rubinsky
Phillip Griebel, crewman

Fort Mercer Stern
Alanson Winn, crewmember
Luis Jomidad, quartermaster
Jesse Bushnell, chief engineer
Hurley Newman, quartermaster
Massie Hunt
John Braknis

Rescuers on the Cutter *Acushnet*
John Joseph, captain
John Mihlbauer
Sid Morris
Harvey Madigan, helmsman
George Mahoney, lieutenant

Rescuers on the Cutter *Eastwind*
Oliver Petersen, captain
Len Whitmore, radio operator
Larry White, ensign
John Courtney
Roland Hoffert
Eugene Korpusik

PART I

CHATHAM LIFEBOAT STATION

Chatham, Massachusetts: February 18, 1952

Boatswain's mate first class Bernie Webber held a mug of hot coffee in his large hands as he stared out the foggy window of the mess hall. He watched with growing curiosity and concern as the storm continued to strengthen outside. A midwinter nor'easter had stalled over New England for the last two days, and Bernie wondered if the worst was yet to come. Windswept snow danced over the shifting sands as large drifts piled up in the front yard of the Chatham Lifeboat Station.

Taking a sip of his coffee, Bernie thought of his young wife, Miriam, in bed with a bad case of the flu at their cottage on Sea View Street. What if there was an emergency? What if she needed help? Would the doctor be able to reach her in this kind of weather? These questions were fraying his nerves, and Bernie fought to put them out of his mind. Instead he tried to picture the local fishermen all huddled around the old wood stove at the Chatham Fish Pier. They would be calling for his help soon as their vessels bobbed up and down on the waves in Old Harbor, straining their lines. *If the storm is this bad now, what will it be like in a few hours when it really gets going?* he thought.

Bernie, however, wouldn't complain about the tough day he was facing. The boatswain's mate first class was only 24 years old, but he had been working at sea for nearly a decade, having first served with the U.S. Maritime Service during WWII. Bernie had followed his brother Bob into the Coast Guard; it was not the kind of life his parents had planned for him. From early childhood, Bernie's father, the associate pastor at the Tremont Temple Baptist Church in Boston, had steered him toward a life in the ministry. The church deacon had even paid for Bernie to attend the Mount Hermon School for Boys, which was 105 miles away from their home in Milton.

Bernie was an outcast in the prep school crowd. He arrived in Greenfield, Massachusetts, a small town hugging the Connecticut River, with serious doubts and wearing his brother's hand-me-down clothes. He was not a strong student, and he privately questioned why he was there. Bernie knew in his heart that he did not want to follow in his father's footsteps. He was thinking about running away from school when fate intervened;

a childhood friend who had crashed his father's car came looking for a place to hide out. Bernie snuck his friend into one of the dorm rooms and swiped food from the school cafeteria for the boy to eat. The two were caught after just a few days, but they did not stick around long enough to face the consequences. Instead they fled to the hills and cornfields surrounding the school before eventually making it back to Milton.

Reverend Bernard A. Webber struggled to understand the actions of his wayward son as young Bernie quit school and continued to drift. A year later, at the age of 16, when World War II was under way, Bernie got an idea that would change the course of his rudderless life. He heard that the U.S. Maritime Service was looking for young men to train. If Bernie could complete the arduous training camp, he could then serve the war effort on a merchant ship. He quickly joined up after his father reluctantly signed his enlistment papers, and he learned the fundamentals of seamanship at the Sheepshead Bay Maritime School in New York.

When he was finished with maritime school, Bernie shipped out on a T2 oil tanker in the South Pacific. During this time, he realized that he would not spend his life in the ministry or at any other job on dry land. Bernie Webber had been born to the sea. He enlisted in the U.S. Coast Guard on February 26, 1946, and was sent to its training station in Maryland. In letters to recruits at the time, the commanding officer of the coast guard training station summed up the life of a coast guardsman this way:

HARD JOBS ARE ROUTINE IN THIS
SERVICE. IN A WAY, THE COAST GUARD
IS ALWAYS AT WAR; IN WARTIME,
AGAINST ARMED ENEMIES OF THE
NATION; AND IN PEACETIME, AGAINST
ALL ENEMIES OF MANKIND AT SEA;
FIRE, COLLISION, LAWLESSNESS,
GALES, ICE, DERELICTS, AND MANY
MORE. THE COAST GUARD, THEREFORE,
IS NO PLACE FOR A QUITTER, OR FOR
A CRYBABY, OR ANYONE WHO CANNOT
KEEP HIS EYE ON THE BALL. IT IS UP
TO *YOU*, AS AN INDIVIDUAL TO PROVE
YOUR WORTH.

~

Ten years had passed, and Bernie was now on duty in Chatham, a tiny outpost at the elbow of Cape Cod. His worth and his mettle had been tested many times in the unforgiving waters off the Cape. It was one of the most dangerous places on the sea, because of the shifting sandbars and enormous waves. In fact, seamen referred to the area as "the graveyard of the Atlantic," and for good reason. The sunken skeletons of more than 3,000 shipwrecks were scattered across the ocean floor from Chatham to Provincetown.

Bernie Webber's first challenge had come during an evening

in 1949, when he responded to a distress call at the Chatham Lifeboat Station. The USS *Livermore* had run aground on Bearse's Shoal, off Monomoy Island. Bernie and a crew took a 38-foot boat over the treacherous shallow area known as Chatham Bar to where the *Livermore* lay with a navy crew stranded on board. The ship rested high up on the shoal and was leaning dangerously on its side. Bernie and the men stayed with the destroyer for the rest of the night as salvage tugs were called in. The next morning, the coast guardsmen assisted in several failed attempts to free the warship before finally achieving success and sending the *Livermore* safely on its way. Bernie smiled as the *Livermore*'s crew cheered him and his crew. The sailors had given him a different reception several hours earlier when they pelted him with apples and oranges because, in their eyes, the rescue mission was taking too long. It was all part of a friendly rivalry between the navy and the coasties.

Yes, the life of a coast guardsman was oftentimes a thankless one, but Bernie would not have traded it for any other job in the world. And now, just after dawn, he gazed out the window of the mess hall, listened to the wind howl, and wondered what the day would bring.

THE *PENDLETON*

Captain John J. Fitzgerald Jr. was new to the *Pendleton*, but he was not new to the unpredictability of the New England weather. Fitzgerald, the son of a sea captain, had taken over command of the 503-foot, 10,448-ton T2 tanker just one month prior. The square-jawed resident of Roslindale, Massachusetts, was familiar with these waters and had a healthy respect for the dangers of the North Atlantic.

The *Pendleton* had departed Baton Rouge, Louisiana, on February 12, bound for Boston. The tanker was fully loaded, carrying 122,000 barrels of kerosene and home heating oil from Texas. Like most tanker crews, the men aboard the *Pendleton* were a mixed lot of old buddies and total strangers. It was also a classic melting pot of races, creeds, and colors.

From the very beginning, it had been a difficult voyage for Fitzgerald and his crew of 40 men. The *Pendleton* had run into a severe storm off Cape Hatteras, North Carolina, and the bad weather had stayed with them like a dark omen on the journey up the coast. Now, five days after their departure, the crew faced its toughest challenge yet, a blizzard that showed no sign of weakening. Nine inches of snow had already fallen in Boston, where an army of 500 city workers used 200 trucks and 35 snow loaders to clear the downtown area and the narrow streets of Beacon Hill. The South Shore of Massachusetts was also taking a pounding as huge waves ripped down 30 feet of seawall in the coastal town of Scituate. Farther south on Cape Cod, more than 4,000 telephones had been knocked out as thick ice and snow brought down one line after another. In Maine, it was even worse. A scheduled snowshoe race had to be canceled in Lewiston because of too much snow.

The *Pendleton* reached the outskirts of Boston Harbor late on the evening of Sunday, February 17. Visibility was poor, and Captain Fitzgerald could not see the beam of Boston Light through the blinding snow. Without the lighthouse beacon to guide them, there was no way Fitzgerald would risk the lives of his crewmen by taking the massive tanker into Boston Harbor and around the 34 islands that dotted the area. Instead, Fitzgerald smartly ordered the *Pendleton* back out to deeper ocean, where the ship could ride out the storm before making port.

As midnight approached, the *Pendleton* found itself caught in the middle of a full gale with arctic winds blowing in every direction. By four A.M., the *Pendleton*, despite trying to hold its position in Cape Cod Bay, was pushed by the winds over the tip of Provincetown just east of Cape Cod. Monstrous seas were now crashing over the stern, but the vessel was riding well. The next two hours would change that. At approximately 5:30 A.M., chief engineer Raymond L. Sybert of Norfolk, Virginia, ordered his crew not to go out over the catwalk leading from bow to stern. He also slowed the ship's speed to just seven knots (about eight miles per hour).

Minutes later, a thunderous roar echoed through the bowels of the ship. The crew felt the gigantic tanker rise out of the turbulent ocean. This was followed by a shudder and an earsplitting crash as the *Pendleton* nosed down.

Eighteen-year-old seaman Charles Bridges of Palm Beach, Florida, was asleep in his bunk before the ship lurched and cracked, but the terrible sound made him bolt to his feet. "I grabbed my pants, shoes, and a life vest, and ran topside," recalled Bridges later. "I went into the mess deck where some of the other men had gathered. The power was out and it was still dark outside, so it was hard to know what was going on. Before anyone could stop me, I grabbed a flashlight and ran up to the catwalk to see what the men on the bow of the ship were doing. I shined the flashlight on the steel floor of the catwalk and quickly followed it amidships. The waves were enormous, and their spray was whipping across the deck, mingling with the cold sleet falling. Then I stopped in my tracks because the catwalk floor disappeared, and I realized just two more steps, and I'd drop straight down into the ocean."

Bridges wheeled around and scurried back to the mess deck, shouting, "We're in trouble! The ship has broke in two!"

Some of the men talked of immediately lowering the lifeboats. But Bridges told them they were crazy, that the lifeboats wouldn't stand a chance in the enormous waves.

Down in the lowest deck of the ship, where the fire room was located, no one knew what had happened. Fireman Frank Fauteux of Attleboro, Massachusetts, feared the worst. Fauteux, a nine-year veteran of the sea, was a large man with thick whiskers that ran across his square jawline, giving him the look of Captain Ahab, the character in *Moby-Dick*. Fauteux felt the *Pendleton* lurch and heard the loud explosion that followed. He fought to brace himself as a more violent lurch rattled the wounded ship. Moments later, Sybert came running into the fire room. "The ship has split in half!" he hollered.

～

Just after the ship had sheared in half, first assistant engineer David Brown, who was on duty in the watch room in the stern of the *Pendleton*, put the engines on dead slow ahead. Moments later, Sybert ordered Brown to cut the engines completely. By now, the entire crew had woken up to the thunderous roar and were scrambling out of their quarters to find out what had happened. Everyone had felt the ship rattle, and many had seen a huge ball of fire. Henry Anderson, a maintenance worker, known as a "wiper," from New Orleans, was lying in his sleeping sack when he felt what he later described as a "big bump." Anderson grabbed his life jacket and ran to the mess deck, where he could see the damage firsthand. "Another fellow and myself got a hammer and nailed the door shut because the water was pouring in," he recalled.

A second wiper, 35-year-old Fred Brown, had been shaken awake in his bunk. When he first heard the earth-shattering sound, Brown thought the *Pendleton* had hit a rock. "I heard a big cracking noise," he said later. "It was like the tearing of a large piece of tin." Brown pulled on his clothes and sprinted up to the deck. He huddled with several of his fellow sailors, forming a human shield against the pounding surf that washed over the stern. Brown was stung by blasts of freezing sea spray as he stood with the other men, stunned at the sight of the ship's bow floating away and disappearing into the driving snow. At the time of the break, Captain Fitzgerald and several of his officers were in the forward bridge house just above the main deck. Now they were gone.

Forty-nine-year-old Wallace Quirey, the ship's third assistant engineer, had seen plenty in his 25 years at sea, but he had never seen or felt anything quite like this before. "I got to the stern, and the waves must have been fifty-five feet high," he recalled. "They swept the boat deck, the highest deck, and came five feet away from breaking right at the top of the mast." Others on board the ship placed the wave height at more than 70 feet.

Quirey located the ship's youngest crewmember, 16-year-old Carroll Kilgore, and offered encouragement as the wind and the waves continued to knock them around. Like Bernie Webber had done nearly a decade before, the wild-haired, gap-toothed Kilgore had joined the merchant marines seeking a life of thrills and adventure. A month later, he now found himself crouched on the stern getting slammed by waves, terribly frightened, on what was his first and possibly last voyage.

The shivering seamen looked on with a flicker of hope as the *Pendleton*'s bow came briefly back into view. The bow brushed against the stern and then drifted away like an apparition, with Captain Fitzgerald and seven of his crewmen aboard. Nearly every member of the ship's command staff was now separated from the rest of the crew. The battered survivors on the stern whispered a prayer for their comrades' safety, and then looked to their ranking officer for guidance and hope.

At just 33 years of age, chief engineer Sybert found himself in charge of the stern section of the *Pendleton*. He mustered the crew, which now consisted of 32 men, and ordered all water-tight doors closed, except for those connecting the fire room to the engine room. Sybert also assigned watch details, including lookout watches at both ends of the boat deck. He then went to assess the damage and saw that the *Pendleton* was spilling its load of home heating oil and kerosene into the sea. The thick black liquid covered the frothy crests of angry swells that rose and fell around the ship.

The *Pendleton* was a T2-SE-A1, commonly known as a T2

tanker. But these ships had gained a more dubious nickname: some critics referred to them as "serial sinkers" and "Kaiser's coffins." The trouble with T2 tankers dated back nearly a decade, to January 16, 1943, when a T2 called the *Schenectady* split in half while still at the dock! The ship had just completed its sea trials and had returned to port at Swan Island, Oregon, when suddenly she cracked across the middle. The center portion of the ship buckled and lifted right out of the water, leaving its bow and stern to settle on the river bottom.

Like the *Schenectady*, the *Pendleton* had been built hastily for the war effort. Constructed in Oregon by the Kaiser Company in 1944, the *Pendleton* now called Wilmington, Delaware, home. By all accounts, she looked sturdy enough. Her length was 503 feet, and she was powered by a turboelectric motor of 6,600 horsepower with a single propeller 11 feet across. But the ship's strong outward appearance concealed the subpar welding methods used in its construction. The hull of the *Pendleton* was most likely put together with "dirty steel" or "tired iron," terms that refer to steel weakened by excess sulfur content. This put the ship at great risk in high waves and frigid waters.

~

Now that the *Pendleton* was torn in two, the strong waves began carrying the stern section of the ship south from Provincetown down the jagged arm of Cape Cod. The bow section was drifting in a nearly identical path, but was moving faster and was farther offshore. The radio room was located in the bow, but Captain Fitzgerald had no way to send an SOS signal. When the ship split in half, the circuit breakers kicked out, leaving the bow without power, heat, or light. Because the tanker had watertight compartments in the cargo area, the halves initially stayed afloat, but there was no way to know for how long that would continue. One advantage the tanker had compared to the more famous lost ship, the *Titanic*, was the way it split in half from beam to beam. With the *Titanic*, the iceberg ripped a long gash in the side of the ship, opening several compartments, while the *Pendleton*'s break was across its middle, compromising fewer compartments than if it had been ripped lengthwise along its hull.

Chief engineer Sybert and his men did retain power on the stern, but had no radio equipment to send a distress message. The crewmembers must have looked at one another with the same question running through their minds. *Who will come to save us?*

THE *FORT MERCER*

About the same time the *Pendleton* split, the *Fort Mercer* was locked in its own battle with the seas off Cape Cod. Captain Frederick Paetzel was not taking any chances with the storm that had overtaken his 503-foot oil tanker. Paetzel kept the *Mercer*'s bow pointed into the rising seas, holding position, prepared to ride out the storm. The captain had guided the ship safely since leaving Norco, Louisiana. Now, just 30 miles southeast of Chatham, he wasn't too far from his final destination of Portland, Maine. He might be delayed by the storm, but rough seas in the North Atlantic during the month of February were not unexpected, and he would bide his time until the storm blew itself out.

The nor'easter, however, showed no signs of weakening, and

instead intensified with each passing hour. By the time a pale hint of light indicated dawn's arrival, mountainous waves had grown to 50 and 60 feet, and the wind approached hurricane strength, hurling a freezing mix of sleet and snow at the vessel. The *Mercer* took a terrible pounding, yet rode the seas as well as could be expected, without any excess pitching or rolling.

At eight A.M., Captain Paetzel heard a sharp crack echo from the innards of his ship. He wasn't immediately sure what had happened. Then oil began spewing over the ocean from the starboard side of the *Mercer*, and he knew the hull had cracked.

Captain Paetzel immediately slowed the vessel's speed. After alerting the rest of his crew about the emergency, he radioed the coast guard for assistance, reporting that his ship's seams had opened up.

Once the coast guard was notified, Paetzel and his crew of 42 men could only pray that the ship would stay together until coast guard cutters arrived. The German-born captain had been at sea since he was 14, but he'd never seen a storm like the one he was caught in, nor had he ever heard the sickening crack of metal giving way to the sea.

~

Approximately 150 miles away, aboard the coast guard cutter *Eastwind*, radio operator Len Whitmore was broadcasting on the radio. A fishing vessel, the *Paolina*, out of New Bedford, Massachusetts, was overdue, and the cutter was involved in the search.

The *Eastwind* was in the last known vicinity of the fishing boat, and Len repeatedly broadcast over the radio, hoping to make contact. Voice communication at the time was rudimentary and could span just 40 or 50 miles. Beyond that range, the only method of communication was Morse code.

Len had learned Morse code when he attended the U.S. Coast Guard radio school in Groton, Connecticut. His entry into the coast guard had been a circuitous one, starting when he was 17. On the spur of the moment, Len, his brother Bob, and a friend named Frank Gendreau Jr. had decided it was time to see the world beyond their hometown of Lynn, Massachusetts. The three young men initially set their eyes on the navy and went to the local recruiting office to enlist. Although Len passed the physical, neither of the other two boys did, and the three of them left the office still civilians. They discussed their next option, and Len's brother decided if the navy wouldn't have them, then maybe the coast guard would. Again, however, Bob and Frank failed the physical while Len passed. Thinking the third time would be a charm, Bob and Frank went to the air force recruiting office and were accepted. Len, however, had his sights on the sea, not the skies. He decided to go it alone and joined the coast guard.

After boot camp, Len attended radio school, and upon graduation, his first long-term assignment was on the *Eastwind*, a 280-foot icebreaker. The morning of February 18 was one Len would never forget. "I had just come on duty in the radio room at eight A.M. and was calling for the *Paolina*, when suddenly I

heard a strong SOS in my earphone. It was the *Fort Mercer*." Len
sat bolt upright, taken aback by the distress call that came out of
the blue. He quickly acknowledged the *Mercer*'s message while
motioning to another coastie to run and get chief radioman
John Harnett. Then he alerted the Coast Guard regional communications station, which at the time was located in Marshfield,
Massachusetts.

Len continued communicating with the *Fort Mercer*, trying
to get the ship's position and determine the nature of the emergency. The tanker's radio operator, John O'Reilly, reported that
it had a crack in the hull, and he gave their approximate position. By this time, Len had notified other coast guard vessels
in the vicinity about the emergency.

Unfortunately, Len learned the *Eastwind* was quite a distance
away from the tanker and knew it would take several hours
to reach them. "The weather was blowing a whole gale, and
the seas were enormous. . . . A lot of our crew was seasick,
but still working. With those seas, I thought it might take us
a whole day to get to the *Mercer*, and by then it might be too
late."

Despite the cutter's 150-mile distance from the *Mercer*, the
Eastwind immediately started steaming for the crippled tanker,
abandoning the search for the *Paolina*. (Only bits of wreckage
from the *Paolina* were ever found.) Oliver Petersen, from Win-
chester, Massachusetts, captain of the *Eastwind*, was put in charge
of the rescue operation. In Provincetown, Massachusetts, the
cutter *Yakutat* was also dispatched to the scene.

~

Aboard the *Fort Mercer*, Captain Paetzel tensed each time a particularly large wind-whipped wave hit the vessel. Paetzel had the crew don life vests, but beyond that safety measure, they could do little besides wait for the coast guard to arrive.

Remarkably, at ten A.M., the *Boston Globe* newspaper was able to make a shore-to-ship telephone connection with the captain. Paetzel said the conditions were very rough and that waves had reached 68 feet, rising up into the rigging. He added that he could not be sure of the situation because surveying the damage more closely from the deck would be suicidal. "We're just standing still," he said. As a final thought, he considered loved ones onshore and expressed a hope that "none of our wives hear about this."

Suddenly, at 10:30 A.M., another terrifying crack rang out, and the ship lurched. Paetzel instantly sent a message to the coast guard explaining that the situation was worsening. A cold sensation of dread coursed through the captain; he knew his ship might become the ninth T2 tanker to be taken by the sea.

The stress on the ship was enormous, especially as one wave lifted the bow and another the stern, leaving no support in the middle. The storm had breached the tanker's welded hull, and the seas seemed intent on lengthening the crack. Captain Paetzel and his crew were helpless.

Another long hour went by without incident. Then at 11:40

A.M., a third loud report was heard as more metal cracked. Captain Paetzel could now see the fissure, with oil spurting into the rampaging seas. At 11:58 A.M., Paetzel had another SOS sent, this one accompanied by the message "Our hull is splitting."

A couple minutes later, a wave smashed the tanker so hard crewmen were thrown to the floor. When they got to their feet, they could not believe what they saw; the vessel had split in two!

Crewmember Alanson Winn said that when the final crack and split occurred, it was so loud and violent he thought the ship had been rammed. "Then she lifted up out of the water like an elevator. She gave two jumps. And when she'd done that, she tore away."

Captain Paetzel was trapped on the bow with eight other men, while the stern held 34 crewmembers, and each end was drifting away from the other. The forward end of the bow rode high in the air, but the aft, or back, section sloped down to the sea, washing away the lifeboats. Equally devastating, the accident had knocked out the radio, and Captain Paetzel could no longer work with the coast guard for rescue. Paetzel and his men were helplessly trapped in the bridge, the compartment where the captain operated the large vessel—to leave might mean instant death. The bow wallowed in the monstrous seas, and without engine power, it was broadside to the waves, taking direct hits.

The stern section, where the engine was located, was in much better shape, and all of it was above the seas. Right after the split, engineers immediately shut the engine down, but now the crew on the stern could see waves pushing the bow back toward them like a battering ram. Frantically, the engineers restarted the engine and put the propeller in reverse. They were able to back the stern away before the bow ran them down. Their troubles, however, were just beginning.

"IT CAN'T BE TRUE . . ."

On board the *Eastwind*, radio operator Len Whitmore was in regular communication with radioman John O'Reilly of the *Mercer*. Len tried to keep the *Mercer* crew encouraged, letting them know that the *Eastwind* and *Yakutat* were en route. The *Eastwind*'s progress into the teeth of the howling gale, however, was incredibly slow, and Len felt frustrated that hours would go by before they could reach the tanker.

With 43 crewmembers of the *Mercer* in danger of losing their lives, coast guard commanders knew they needed boats on the scene as quickly as possible. They reacted by dispatching motor lifeboats from Chatham and Nantucket. Sending 36-foot motor lifeboats into seas twice their size had to be a difficult decision—the lifeboats and their crews might be the next victims of the storm.

The first motor lifeboat sent into the maelstrom left from Brant Point Station, Nantucket. In command was chief boatswain's mate Ralph Ormsby with a crew of three: Alfred Roy, Donald Pitts, and John Dunn. The four men had 55 dangerous miles to navigate to reach the *Mercer*'s halves, and their boat motored into waves so large that they often washed over the crew.

Almost immediately, the boat was in trouble. "Roy, who was at the wheel," said Ormsby, "was thrown off of it. I seized it. The boat stood almost on end with the waves breaking over her bow. We spotted the waves before they hit to guide the course of the boat."

A second 36-foot motor lifeboat was ordered out of Chatham. Station commander Daniel W. Cluff received orders to send the boat out, and he in turn told Chief Donald Bangs of Scituate, Massachusetts, to select a crew and head to the *Mercer*. Bangs quickly chose a crew consisting of engineer Emory Haynes, boatswain's mate Antonio Ballerini, and seaman Richard Ciccone.

When Bernie Webber heard the orders, he thought, *My God, do they really think a lifeboat and its crew can make it that far out to sea in this storm with only a compass to guide them?* Webber figured that even if the crew didn't freeze to death, they would never be able to get men off the storm-tossed sections of the *Mercer*.

Bernie was friends with these men and wondered if he'd ever see them alive again.

Webber's concern that the men might freeze to death was an all-too-realistic prospect. One of the body's first responses to fight the onset of hypothermia is to decrease the blood flow to the limbs and thereby reduce heat loss from the body's extremities, especially the feet and hands. Reduced blood flow to the limbs aids the body's efforts to maintain core heat, which is essential for the main organs, especially the heart. But the decreased blood flow to the hands, arms, and feet comes at a cost—the ability to perform tasks. Should the lifeboat's motor die, the men on board would not have the dexterity in their fingers to solve the problem. Hands and feet would also suffer frostbite. And in 1952, before the days of neoprene gloves and polypropylene inner wear, the crews had nothing to protect their skin other than rubberized foul-weather gear.

Both Ormsby's and Bang's crews would be tested by the frigid sea and air—if their boats did not capsize first and end their lives.

~

Airplanes took to the stormy skies from the coast guard air station at Salem, Massachusetts, and from the naval air base at Quonset Point, Rhode Island. One of the planes arrived before the cutters at approximately two P.M. Pilot George Wagner radioed, "The tanker has definitely hove to. Her stern is into the wind and almost awash." He also reported that the *Mercer*'s lifeboats were gone. The pilot flew his plane downwind, searching for the lifeboats, but found none.

About the same time the airplanes arrived on the scene, station commander Cluff and boatswain's mate "Chick" Chase were in Chatham's watchtower at the radar screen. Earlier in the day, the radar had malfunctioned, but now it was fixed, and the first thing they saw on the screen were two strange objects. "The objects," recalled Chase, "were just five miles offshore, nowhere near where the *Mercer* was supposed to be. I wondered how the *Mercer* could have drifted so far, and we realized something wasn't right." Cluff immediately called headquarters, and they in turn alerted George Wagner, who was still flying above the stern of the *Mercer*.

Wagner, struggling to control his plane in the storm, wondered what in the world this perplexing message was all about. He was staring down at the *Mercer*'s stern and thought it impossible that its bow could have drifted over 25 miles toward Chatham. And what did it mean that Chatham radar picked up two targets? All Wagner could do was bank his plane and head west to take a look. Fortunately, the snow had turned mostly to rain and sleet, and visibility had improved a bit.

Wagner flew at a low altitude and was buffeted by the wind but quickly made it to the known landmark of the Pollock Rip Lightship, a stationary vessel used like a floating lighthouse. Incredibly, not far from the lightship was the broken half of a tanker's bow. Wagner noticed that the superstructure on the bow below was brown, a different color than the white superstructure on the stern he had come from. He shook his head in disbelief and circled around for another look. Then his jaw dropped. On the bow, in large white lettering, was the name *Pendleton*! When he radioed what he had seen, everyone in the coast guard was stunned. It was almost too much to believe that a second vessel, just 30 miles from the *Mercer*, had also split in two.

Eastwind radioman Len Whitmore sat in astonishment, wondering if he had heard the pilot's words correctly. *Another tanker?* Up to this point, no one had even mentioned the name *Pendleton*. Len thought, *It can't be true. There must be some mistake.*

"YOU GOT TO TAKE THE *36500* OUT"

Before the *Pendleton* was spotted, Bernie Webber had already put in a busy morning. Several fishing boats had broken their moorings and lay scattered on the shore at Old Harbor. Webber and crew used the motor lifeboat *CG 36500* to help the fishermen pull the boats off the beach and reattach them to their moorings before the surf damaged them. It was a mariner's version of herding cattle, but instead of working under the hot Texas sun, they had to perform their task in blinding snow and bone-chilling temperatures.

Webber was assisted by seaman Richard Livesey and a long-time friend, engineman first class Mel Gouthro, who was battling the flu in addition to the elements. The nor'easter reminded Livesey of the 14 months he had spent on an icebreaker in the northern Atlantic. At age 22, he was a couple of years younger than Webber, but, like his boss, what Livesey lacked in age, he made up for in experience.

Richard Livesey was born in South Boston, Massachusetts, in 1930 but was raised 58 miles south in Fairhaven, a fishing village on the shore of Buzzard's Bay. Livesey was steered toward a life at sea early on, thanks to the countless stories told to him by his father, Oswald, who had spent 22 years as a chief water tender in the U.S. Navy.

Livesey was one of those young men who seemed to have salt water coursing through his veins. He had wanted to join the navy for as long as he could remember, and when he was old enough, he asked his father to accompany him to the recruiting office. "Sure," said the elder Livesey, beaming that his son was carrying on the seaman tradition.

Their excitement flickered out briefly when the recruiter informed them that there was a ten-month wait for enlistment. It was 1947, and Richard Livesey was 17 years old. Ten months felt like a lifetime to an anxious teenager who was eager for action and adventure. As they walked out of the recruiting office, Richard told his father he would join the U.S. Air Force instead. At that moment, they noticed a sign for the coast guard recruiting office just a few doors down. The teenager's hopes for an adventure at sea were not dashed after all.

Livesey had only one question for the recruiter. "When can I get shipped out?" he asked. "Tomorrow," barked the man. Livesey signed up on the spot but did not ship out the next day as promised. Instead, he had to wait a full week before heading off to boot camp.

Grinding his way through boot camp, Richard counted the days until he could go to sea. He spent the next four years serving on coast guard cutters and icebreakers around the United States before finding his way onto a patrol boat at the New Bedford station. He left the coast guard briefly in 1951 after his enlistment period was over. He first tried his hand at road construction and then working in a few fish plants. The pay was better, but the jobs lacked the excitement he had experienced in the coast guard, so he reenlisted. Now here he was, retying fishing boats to their moorings on this brutal Monday morning in mid-February.

When the work was completed, Webber, Livesey, and Gouthro secured the motor lifeboat to its mooring, then hopped in the dory, a small boat used for transportation to and from larger vessels, and headed to shore. The men were exhausted, hungry, and cold, and could not wait to get back to the Chatham Lifeboat Station for a hot meal and a change of clothes. The ice-cold seawater had soaked through their foul-weather gear right into their aching bones. Gouthro was shaking from both the cold and the flu he was suffering from.

As the tired men paused on the Chatham Fish Pier to survey their work, a coast guard truck pulled up alongside.

"Get over to Orleans and Nauset beach," the driver yelled. "There's a shipwreck offshore, and they need help." Ground confirmation of the *Pendleton*'s plight came from a woman living in the Nauset inlet. She had heard the ship's horn sounding seven times offshore.

Webber and crew were instructed to join the Nauset Lifeboat Station crew in their amphibious vehicle to try to locate the tanker and give aid if possible. The Duck, as it was called because its manufacturing code was DUKW, was a six-wheel-drive amphibious military truck developed during World War II. It was most prominently used during the Allied invasion of Normandy on D-day. And now, used by the coast guard at Nauset Beach, the Duck was the perfect vehicle to carry the coasties over the sand and through shoreline surf as they hunted for the drifting *Pendleton*. But first Webber and crew had to get to Orleans.

The drive up the arm of Cape Cod on snow-covered Route 28 to Orleans was a white-knuckle ride for the three coasties. Under the snow lay a sheet of ice, and their Dodge truck pressed ahead slowly along the winding road. Fortunately, the heater in the truck was working, but the comfort only made Webber think about his friend Donald Bangs, who was out in the icy ocean, hopefully still alive.

Webber, Livesey, and Gouthro finally reached Orleans and met the rest of the crew from the Nauset Lifeboat Station. The men piled into a Duck and continued on to Nauset Beach, where they parked at a hill. At any other time, the hill would have provided them with a perfect vantage point to scan miles of shoreline. But the high perch offered no help on this day because the shoreline had virtually disappeared. The seas were now running over the beach, across the parking lot, and halfway up the hill. However, after a few moments, the snow abated briefly and the men were able to spot a gray hulk, an object darker than the ocean, rolling rapidly along the towering waves. It was half a ship, drifting swiftly south toward Chatham!

The coast guardsmen knew there was no way the Duck could catch her now. Bernie, Richard, and Mel immediately started back to the Chatham Lifeboat Station.

Meanwhile, the coast guard issued a directive to all the ships currently involved in the *Fort Mercer* rescue operation. The alert was classified "operational immediate" and was printed in bold type:

DEFINITE INDICATION THAT TANKER *PENDLETON* HAS BROKEN IN TWO—STERN SECTION IN BREAKERS OFF CHATHAM—BOW SECTION DRIFTING NEAR POLLOCK RIP LV—NO PRIOR INDICATION REGARDING CASUALTY TO *PENDLETON—PENDLETON* DUE IN BOSTON YESTERDAY AND NOT ARRIVED—THIS IN ADDITION TO *FORT MERCER.*

~

Back at the Chatham Lifeboat Station, the nasty weather had kept engineer Andy "Fitz" Fitzgerald inside the relative warmth of the station's "motor-mack shack." The 20-year-old was the youngest coast guardsman at the station. Fitz was not born to the sea, and in fact, he hadn't even become a strong swimmer until he joined the guard. He grew up in Whitinsville, Massachusetts, and while attending high school in the 1940s, he played football. At 140 pounds, he was an undersized linebacker, but he loved the competition.

This period was a bleak time in Whitinsville and the surrounding Blackstone Valley. The mighty mills along the Blackstone River that had given lifeblood to the Industrial Revolution during the 19th century were dying. When Fitzgerald graduated from high school, he had no money for college and no prospects for a future in Whitinsville. This prompted him and a friend to hitchhike to the local train station, ride into Boston, and join the coast guard.

Part of Fitzgerald's morning duty in Chatham was to row out to the station's three boats. He would make sure that each vessel's tank was topped off with gasoline, and he would also start their engines and give them a good running before returning to shore. On this morning, Chatham Lifeboat Station's new commanding officer, Daniel Cluff, had ordered Fitzgerald to stand down. The storm had become too severe to risk sending the young engineer out in a tiny rowboat.

~

Late afternoon was giving way to the darkness of evening as an exhausted Bernie Webber and crew continued driving back to

Chatham Station. Webber needed to inform Cluff that the stern section of the *Pendleton* was heading their way fast.

Arriving at the station, Webber found his boss pacing the floor, trying to decide the best course of action. This was the first big emergency of Cluff's tenure as commander at Chatham Station. Some coasties wondered if he was up to the challenge.

Daniel Cluff was a native of Chincoteague, Virginia, a small fishing village on Virginia's eastern shore and home to the famous Chincoteague Pony Swim. The commanding officer had spent little time involved in the boat work of the station, thinking he needed first to get to know the town's business leaders.

Cluff called Webber toward him and in his Southern drawl said, "Webber, pick yourself a crew. You got to take the *36500* out over the bar and assist that ship, ya hear?"

Bernie felt his heart drop to his feet. He could picture himself trying to steer the tiny wooden rescue boat over the hazardous Chatham Bar and into the high seas. The bar is a collection of ever-shifting shoals of sand, which lie only a few feet below the surface. When swells, formed in the deep ocean, hit the bar, they become steep and their tops break off, crashing with incredible force. One cubic yard of water weighs nearly 1,700 pounds; when that force hits a vessel, the boat can splinter in a matter of seconds. And there was no way to avoid the bar. Because of the way nature had designed the channel, there was only one way in and one way out. Bernie and his men had to cross the bar.

The images of the bar burned in Bernie's memory as he received Cluff's orders. He immediately thought of the coast guard's official motto, *Semper Paratus*, Latin for "Always Ready." However, it was the unofficial coast guard motto that now weighed heavily in his mind: *You have to go out, but you do not have to come back.*

"Yes, Mr. Cluff," Webber replied. "I'll get ready."

Privately, Bernie wondered why he had been chosen for this dangerous mission when there were equally seasoned officers on duty. Still, he accepted without hesitation. Now he needed some like-minded men to follow his lead. "Who'll come with me?" he asked aloud.

Richard Livesey was more than a little concerned. He had seen the mighty waves crashing over North Beach and knew such a mission would be horrendous. Still, he fought the fear, fatigue, and cold running through his body and raised his hand. "Bernie, I'll go with you," he said.

Andy Fitzgerald was also in the room and said, "Mel's as sick as a dog. I'll go." Fitz had been fighting boredom all day and was eager to volunteer.

The crew was still in need of a fourth man. Ervin Maske was hanging around in the mess hall when he heard Webber's call. Maske was a guest at the station and easily could have said no to the mission. The 23-year-old native of Marinette, Wisconsin, was a member of the Stonehorse Lightship. He had just returned from leave and was awaiting transport back to his ship, which was stationed about a mile off the southeast tip of Monomoy Point.

Like Webber, Maske also had a wife waiting for him at

home. He was newly married to the former Florence Silverman, whom he had met at a dance hall in Brooklyn. He had much to lose, and not much to gain, on this operation with a crew he had never met before. Still, he volunteered for the rescue mission without a second of uncertainty. Webber shook Maske's hand and told him to get ready.

The crew of four was ready and willing, but were they able? Webber, at just 24 years of age, was the oldest of the group and the most experienced. The others were in their early 20s, and Andy was fresh out of engineman school training. He had never been on a rescue but had heard about the difficulties of crossing Chatham Bar in high seas. The engineman hoped that his lack of experience would not be a detriment to the crew. Although he didn't know Bernie very well on a personal level—with Bernie being older and married—Andy had been on the *CG 36500* with Bernie during routine duty. If Andy could have chosen any man at the station to navigate the lifeboat over the bar and into the surrounding waters during a storm, he would have picked Bernie. But this was no ordinary storm. Andy had been listening to the various reports coming in on the marine radio, and they were talking about unimaginable seas, in some cases over 60 feet.

Maske, Webber, Fitzgerald, and Livesey had never trained as a unit, and in fact, the three crewmen from Chatham had never even met Maske until that day. But the foursome had as many similarities as differences. All were in great physical shape, and all had joined the coast guard to save lives—now was their chance. Webber was the tallest, at six foot two, with a lanky build and a reserved demeanor. Livesey, about four inches shorter, had a happy-go-lucky outlook with a good sense of humor. Andy, just short of six feet tall, had a ready smile and made friends wherever he went. Maske, the shortest of the group, was a relatively quiet young man, but certainly one with gumption—not many men would put their lives at risk by volunteering to go into a maelstrom with strangers. All four felt gripped by fear, thinking of the storm-tossed seas, but each mustered the determination to keep his anxiety in check and do what had to be done.

BLOWOUT AT CHATHAM BAR

With great trepidation, Webber, Livesey, Fitzgerald, and Maske departed the Chatham Lifeboat Station and drove back down to the Chatham Fish Pier. Webber parked the Dodge truck and stepped out into the snow. Through the thick snowflakes, the crew could barely see the small wooden lifeboat they would be taking on their journey, rocking violently back and forth in the distance. The coast guardsmen walked to the side of the pier and climbed down a ladder and into a small dory. They were getting it ready to row out when Webber heard a voice call from the pier above them. "You guys better get lost before you get too far out," cried local fisherman John Stello. It was his way of saying "turn back while you still can."

Stello and Webber had become close friends over the past

couple of years. The two lived across from each other on Sea View Street. "Call Miriam and tell her what's going on!" Webber shouted back.

Bernie had not spoken to his wife in two days. He thought of her home sick in bed, and his heart ached. Webber looked into the faces of the three other men in the dory, wondering how they'd hold up in the hours to come. He thought back to his wife again and hoped she would be able to cope if he didn't make it home. Bernie could handle risking his own life on what looked to be a suicide mission, but a wave of emotion swept over him when he thought of the life he had begun to build with Miriam.

~

Bernie and Miriam's relationship had been one of great persistence, especially on her part. It had begun over the phone two years earlier. Webber and a couple of his mates had taken his 1939 Plymouth two-door sedan up to Provincetown for a date with three local girls. They had made it as far as Orleans when the car suddenly broke down. Webber walked until he found a pay phone and called his date to explain the mishap. His night on the town was ruined.

Webber had the old Plymouth towed back to Chatham. A few nights later, a young woman called the Chatham Lifeboat Station looking for a gentleman named Webb. As it turned out, the woman had the wrong name but the right man. Bernie grabbed the phone and began talking to this mystery woman, who wouldn't offer her name or anything else about herself. She playfully told him that she had seen him before and that she knew who he was.

The game played on over several more telephone conversations as Webber's curiosity continued to grow. During their long talks on the phone, he found it strange that she would constantly interrupt him. "Wait a sec," she would tell him before leaving the line for a few moments. The mystery was solved when the woman finally told Webber that she was a telephone operator in nearby Wellfleet. In fact, she was the operator who had patched Webber's phone call through to his date on the night his car had broken down on the way to Provincetown.

Bernie and Miriam eventually married and made a life together in Chatham. But their marriage was coupled with a dangerous job, and a price had to be paid for such happiness.

~

As the crew rowed out into the harbor, Webber sized up the *CG 36500*, which appeared to be staring back at him in the distance. Much would be expected of this wooden lifeboat. The lives of his three crewmembers, whoever was still alive aboard the stern section of the *Pendleton*, and the children he planned to have with Miriam all depended on it. *Are you up to the challenge, old girl?* he wondered.

Like all lifeboats of its shape and size, the *CG 36500* had been built at the U.S. Coast Guard Yard in Curtis Bay, Maryland. She was 36 feet, eight inches long with a ten-foot beam and a three-foot draft. The boat weighed a solid 20,000 pounds and was self-righting and self-bailing, thanks to its 2,000-pound bronze keel. The double-ended vessel had been designed to withstand just about anything Mother Nature could put in its way, although Bernie wondered whether its builders had contemplated a winter hurricane like the one that was now pounding the coast of New England.

~

Webber and his crew finally reached the *CG 36500* and climbed aboard. They secured the dory to the buoy and settled in for the arduous journey ahead. Webber, Fitzgerald, and Livesey were all familiar with the lifeboat. Webber took his position in the wheelman's shelter, and they departed; it was 5:55 P.M. The sky had gone from charcoal gray to pitch-black. The lights onshore grew smaller as the four men made their way across Chatham Harbor.

The crew could now see the waves breaking on North Beach. Each man was weighing the possibilities for getting over Chatham Bar. Webber tied a long leather belt around his waist and fastened himself to the wheelman's shelter. The *CG 36500* made a turn in the channel, where the men were met by the sweeping beam of Chatham Lighthouse. In the distance, Webber could see dim lights glowing in the main building. *What's going on in there?* he wondered. For a moment, he prayed that he would get a call on the radio ordering him to turn back. Webber grabbed the radio and called the station, giving Cluff an update, hoping for a change in orders.

"Proceed as directed," Cluff responded with his Virginia twang.

Webber and crew pushed on. They were already fighting the severe cold; their tired feet felt like blocks of ice inside their buckled rubber overshoes. Reaching the end of Chatham Harbor, the men heard the roaring at the bar, where the crashing waves created acres of yellowish white foam.

This is not going to be a good trip, Richard Livesey thought. As the tumultuous sound at the bar became louder, Livesey had the distinct feeling he was experiencing his last minutes on earth. Andy Fitzgerald, who manned the searchlight mounted on the forward turtlebacked compartment, also felt trepidation as the torturous roaring of the breakers became louder. He was putting his faith in Bernie's experience and in the construction of the *CG 36500.* Andy had always thought of the lifeboat as a floating tank—slow but seaworthy, no matter what the weather. Now this little tank was the only thing that stood between him and the frigid ocean.

As they motored ever closer, the searchlight partially illuminated the shoals of the bar, and all four men caught a glimpse of what was ahead. Webber could not believe the height of the seas and thought his boat seemed smaller than ever. Scared and nearly freezing to death, Webber was forced to make a decision that could very well cost the lives of his crewmen. *Do I turn back? Do I go ahead? What do I do now?*

Webber knew that he would not be criticized for turning back. Why add to the tragedy by sending four more men to their deaths on Chatham Bar? He cleared his head and turned his thoughts to the men he was attempting to save. In his mind's eye, Bernie could picture the *Pendleton* crew trapped inside that giant steel casket. He and his crew were their only hope.

~

Webber's thoughts drifted back two years to another rescue attempt he had made in equally hazardous conditions. So haunted was he by the tragedy that he could almost see the faces of those lost men on the crest of each rising wave. Like the *Pendleton*, the New Bedford–based scalloper *William J. Landry* had also found itself trapped by a fearsome nor'easter.

That storm had hit in the early spring of 1950. Heavy snow fell in a curtain off Cape Cod, and the angry storm was aggravated by 70-mile-per-hour winds and rough seas. The *William J. Landry* was taking on water while attempting to circle Monomoy toward Nantucket Sound. During this crisis, Captain Arne Hansen managed to send out a distress call that was received by the Pollock Rip Lightship and relayed back to the Chatham Lifeboat Station.

Bernie Webber had been part of a four-man crew led by veteran seaman Frank Masachi. They were ordered to take out the motor lifeboat *36383*, which was moored in Stage Harbor, but just getting to the lifeboat would prove to be a life-and-death struggle. The normally tranquil Stage Harbor was topped by a blanket of menacing whitecaps that offered a visible warning for sane men to stay ashore.

The crew fitted the small dory with thole pins to hold the oars in place and then dragged it to water's edge. They pushed the vessel out and helped one another get aboard. Webber and Mel Gouthro grabbed the oars and began their battle against the turbulent seas while Masachi and Antonio Ballerini sat low in the boat. The small dory began taking on water almost immediately as it struggled toward the lifeboat.

Suddenly the dory capsized, throwing Webber and the others into the bone-chilling water. The coast guardsmen kicked off their heavy boots, grabbed the bottom of the overturned boat, and held on. Gradually, the waves pushed the boat to shore, where it beached itself on Morris Island, across from Stage Harbor.

Webber and the other crewmen had hoped to seek refuge in an old boathouse but, fighting back the frigid cold crawling up his legs, Masachi refused to give up the mission. He ordered his men to right the 19-foot dory, find the oars, and resume the journey toward the *CG 36383*. Their valiant effort came up short once more; this time the thole pins snapped, capsizing the boat and sending the men back into the icy water. Again, they managed to make it back to Morris Island, where they finally opted to get warm inside the boathouse.

The crew rubbed their aching arms and legs and started the old Kohler gasoline-powered generator. Frank Masachi cranked the antiquated magneto telephone connecting him to the Chatham Station and was told that the *William J. Landry* was still afloat, but taking on massive amounts of water. Knowing that the fishing crew were alive seemed to reenergize him. He decided they would make a third attempt to reach the lifeboat.

Webber and the rest of the crew found some broom handles and whittled them down to replace the broken thole pins. Again, the tired, frozen men walked on sore legs down the beach to the frigid water. Again, they were turned back—this time the oars broke before the vessel plunged them into the sea. They struggled to Morris Island, utterly exhausted and freezing cold, then waded back to Chatham Station.

At this time, the crew aboard the Pollock Rip Lightship finally had the *Landry* in their sights. That was the good news. The bad news was that the storm was intensifying and the seas were at top heights. As the *Landry* crew was attempting to retrieve the towing rope from the lightship, a mighty wave slammed the vessels together, further damaging the fishing dragger. After 24 hours of fighting for their lives, the *Landry*'s crew were now physically and emotionally beaten.

Lightship skipper Guy Emro had been speaking to Captain Hansen over the radio and heard the captain say, "Oh my God," and then nothing else.

When Hansen came back on the radio, he said they were giving up the fight. The last wave had been a dagger in the heart of the crew. "We're going down below to pray and have something to eat," the exhausted captain reported. "If we die out here, it will be with full stomachs. So long, thank you. God bless you all."

Guy Emro reported the news to Chatham Station and then watched as the seas swallowed the *William J. Landry* whole. The remains of the crew were never found.

The tragedy left a bitter taste in Bernie Webber's mouth. He had tried but failed to save the lives of those doomed fishermen. Now, less than two years later, he was faced with a similar, desperate challenge.

As he peered out at the ominous Chatham Bar, the only obstacle between them and the open sea, Bernie Webber had an epiphany. He believed that God had placed him in this time and in this place. He thought about the iron will of Frank Masachi, and he also thought back to the thousands of sermons he had heard his father give while he was growing up. They had all been preparing him for this. He pictured the disappointment in his father's eyes when he had turned his back on the ministry as an aimless youth. On this stormy night, Bernie believed that he was serving God. Webber later recalled the feeling. "You receive the strength and the courage, and you know what your duty is. You realize that you have to attempt a rescue. It's born in you; it is part of your job."

As the lifeboat pitched along a canyon of waves, Webber and

his crew spontaneously began to sing. They sang out of a combination of determination and fear through the snow and freezing sea spray. Their four voices formed a harmony that rose over the howling winds. Webber could think of no more poignant hymn to fit the situation they found themselves in.

Rock of Ages, cleft for me,
Let me hide myself in Thee;
Let the water and the blood,
From Thy wounded side which flowed,
Be of Sin the double cure;
Save from wrath and make me pure.

The men grew silent as Webber motored the *CG 36500* into the bar. The searchlight cut through the snow and darkness, and Andy could see—and feel—that the waves were growing and swirling from every direction. He braced himself for the collision he knew was coming.

When they hit the bar, the tiny wooden lifeboat cut into a mammoth 60-foot wave. The mountain of bone-chilling water lifted the vessel, tossing it into the air like a small toy. All the men were temporarily airborne.

The boat and the men came crashing back down on the hard surface of the sea, and another huge wave struck. This time, a torrent of water washed over the crew, knocking them to the deck. The violent wave shattered the boat's windshield, sending shards of glass into Webber's face and hair as he fell backward.

The wave had spun the *CG 36500* completely around, and its bow was now facing the shore. It was the most dangerous position for the boat and the crew. Webber pulled himself up off the deck and attempted to steer the boat back into the seas before it broached and killed them all. He brushed bits of glass off his face with one hand, the other gripped firmly on the steering wheel. With the windshield now broken, the sea spray came into the wheelman's shelter, pelting Webber's flesh with ice and picking at his open wounds. The snow was hitting his face so hard he could barely open his eyes. As he tried to get his bearings, he glanced down to where the boat's compass should have been. The compass—his sole means of navigation—was gone, torn from its mount. He had to rely on instinct alone.

Blindly, Webber pointed the boat back toward the oncoming wave. When the wave hit, Livesey had the sensation that the little lifeboat was being consumed by the wall of salt water. He could feel that the boat was on its side, and for a sickening second, he wondered if it would right itself.

The wave freed the boat from its grip. Webber used every ounce of strength and again straightened the vessel. He gave it throttle, advancing a few more precious feet. Seconds later, another wave slammed into the vessel, again sending it careening on its side at a 45-degree angle.

Webber managed to get the lifeboat back under control. Then, despite the crashing of the ocean, each man realized one sound was missing. The motor had died, and the next wave was bearing down on them.

CHATHAM MOBILIZES

In an odd coincidence, the front page of the February 18, 1952, edition of the *New York Times* ran an article about World War II tankers. It had nothing to do with the drama that was unfolding off the coast of Chatham. The article described how "nationally known individuals turned a $100,000 investment into a $2,800,000 profit by buying and chartering five World War II tankers." The Senate investigations subcommittee would begin public hearings involving the tankers and corruption in government.

The days of instant reporting had not yet arrived, and so far the only people who were well informed of the double tanker disaster were those in the coast guard and the private citizens of Chatham.

Ed Semprini finished a long day in the broadcast booth at Cape Cod radio station WOCB. He had just returned home when he received a call from fellow journalist Lou Howes. "Don't bother sitting down for dinner," Howes advised his friend. "We've got a tanker that went down off Chatham." Before Semprini could respond, Howes added to the graveness of the situation. "There's not one tanker," he said. "There's two of them! I'm heading to the Chatham Lifeboat Station right now."

"How about giving me a ride?" Semprini asked. "I'll go down with you." Semprini hung up the phone and then called his engineer Wes Stidstone. "Gather your equipment and meet me in Chatham," Semprini told him. "I think we've got a big story on our hands."

Semprini's wife, Bette, overheard the conversation and looked out the window at the driving snow illuminated under the streetlight. "You've got to go out on a night like this?" she asked with worry in her voice. Semprini nodded wearily and then put on his wool coat and hat, wondering what the evening had in store.

~

Lou Howes pulled up in front of Semprini's home and honked the horn. The horn and the engine seemed to be the only instruments that were in good working order in the battered old

Chevrolet. Semprini heard the blare of the horn and trudged through the snow toward his ride. He climbed into the passenger side and rubbed his cold hands in front of the heater, which he quickly realized was broken. *This trip better be worth it*, the newsman thought to himself as the jalopy pulled away from his house and into the blinding snow.

While the blizzard wailed outside, Cape Codders stayed in their warm homes and huddled around the radio as news of the rescue missions began to spread. Those with shortwave radios could listen in real time to the dramatic dispatches between the coast guard station and the rescue crews.

Chatham's town fathers found out about the drama that was unfolding off their coast during their annual budget meeting that night. Members were slowly filing in and had had just enough time to shake the snow off their winter coats before they were told of the dire situation involving the seamen. The town's business would have to wait. Professional photographer Dick Kelsey immediately realized the importance of what was happening. He raced home and grabbed his old 4x5 Speed Graphic camera, #2 flashbulbs, and several film holders and headed for the fish pier.

If the rescue crews somehow made it back alive, they would be cold, hungry, and possibly very sick. The call went out to the town clothier to gather up warm clothes. The local representative of the Red Cross was also alerted. Ordinary men and women went home and began cooking warm meals for the seamen in hopes they would return. The people of Chatham had been raised on the sea, and they knew what needed to be done.

The town's dependence on the sea went back to its founding father, who had purchased the land that would later become Chatham with a boat. William Nickerson, a weaver from Norfolk, England, was the first to settle here. In 1665, Nickerson offered a shallop boat to the Monomoyick sachem Mattaquason in exchange for four square miles of rugged land on which to build his homestead. To seal the deal, Nickerson also threw in 12 axes, 12 hoes, 12 knives, and 40 shillings in wampum, among other items.

This was a harsh land, with strong, howling coastal winds. The settlers built their dwellings with low roofs to withstand hurricanes and blizzards and faced the structures south for maximum exposure to the sun. They insulated the walls with dried seaweed.

By the time of the Revolutionary War, many of the men of Chatham had begun fishing in the waters off the coast. With fishing came shipwrecks. The Humane Society of the Commonwealth of Massachusetts was the first organized group to offer aid to shipwrecked men, building huts along remote sections of the coast to provide shelter for survivors once they made it to shore.

In 1847, Congress finally took action to better protect seamen by appropriating thousands of taxpayer dollars to build permanent lifesaving stations along America's vast coastlines. It would take another 27 years before the first government-authorized lifesaving stations were erected on Cape Cod. In all, nine stations were built from Race Point in Provincetown to Monomoy Island in Chatham. Chatham Station was one of the original nine lifesaving stations built on Cape Cod, its patrol covering more than four miles north and south. The station was equipped with four surfboats, a dory, two beach carts, and a horse named Baby that was used to haul lifesaving equipment down the beach toward disabled vessels.

The Chatham coast was as busy as it was dangerous. Mariners had to concern themselves not only with deadly shoals but also the tricks of men looking to steal their goods. These men were called mooncussers, and they set out to disorient captains and ground their ships by aggressively waving a lantern from the dunes. The mooncussers wanted the captains to think the waving lantern was a legitimate beacon so they would steer their ships into dangerous waters. They hoped that the ships would crash and their goods be strewn about the shore—so they could be easily scavenged. The mooncussers cared only about themselves, and their actions put the lives of many sailors at risk.

The mooncussers got their nickname because they "cussed" the moon on moonlit evenings. They could pull off their dangerous treachery only when the sky was near pitch-black. The writer Henry David Thoreau became fascinated by the mysterious mooncussers during several trips he made to Cape Cod between 1849 and 1857. "We soon met one of these wreckers, a regular Cape Cod man . . . with a bleached and weather-beaten face, within whose wrinkles I distinguished no particular feature.

It was like an old sail endowed with life," Thoreau wrote. "He looked . . . too grave to laugh, too tough to cry; as indifferent as a clam. . . . He was looking for wrecks, old logs . . . bits of boards and joists. . . . When the log was too large to carry far, he cut it up where the last wave had left it, or rolling it a few feet, appropriated it by sticking two sticks into the ground crosswise above it."

The scavenger tradition, though not the deliberate shipwrecking, continued for another hundred years. By the 1950s, the wooden bones of old wrecks could still be found on the beaches of Chatham, disappearing and then reappearing in the shifting sands. One local resident, 82-year-old "Good" Walter Eldridge, had built himself a cottage with wood taken from the wrecks of 17 different vessels that met their fates on Chatham Bar.

And now the citizens of Chatham hoped and prayed that the *CG 36500* carrying Bernie Webber and crew would not add its wooden ribs and planks to the debris on the sands of the bar.

"HE CAME TO THE SURFACE FLOATING"

About the same time that Chatham was mobilizing and Bernie and his crew were being hammered at Chatham Bar, the *Eastwind* was pounding north toward the broken halves of the *Fort Mercer*. Darkness was closing in, and the violent motion aboard the ship was unlike anything radioman Len Whitmore had experienced.

Len wondered if the broken sections of the *Mercer* would remain upright or even stay afloat until his cutter arrived. He had not left the cramped confines of the radio room since eight A.M., and the stress was mounting with each hour. But even in the anxious situation, there was a lighter moment. The cutter's captain was in the radio shack attempting to call the owners of the *Mercer*, when suddenly a pigeon strutted out from behind one of the transmitters and walked casually past the incredulous captain. Len was mortified—it was his pigeon. While the cutter was in New York, Len had found the pigeon with its wing broken, and he snuck it on board, where he planned to nurse it back to health. The captain looked at each man in the room, and they all remained quiet. Len waited for the captain to demand who had brought the bird onto his ship, but instead he went back to his task of connecting with the *Mercer*'s owners. Len let out a silent sigh of relief.

Len wondered how the *Mercer*'s men were holding up. He knew that they were encouraged to learn the coast guard had heard the Mayday and were responding, but that alone did not mean salvation.

~

By 6:30 P.M., the cutter *Yakutat,* commanded by J. W. Naab of Yarmouth, Maine, arrived at the bow section of the *Mercer.* In addition to the seas, wind, and snow, the rescue was now hindered by darkness. Overhead, an airplane from the naval air station at Floyd Bennett Field in Brooklyn, New York, dropped flares, doing its best to provide a little light for the men working below.

Captain Naab's men tried to shoot lines across to the tanker, but the wind made it nearly impossible. *Yakutat* crewman Gil Carmichael later recalled how bitter cold it was as he assisted in trying to get a line to the tanker. "The hood of my parka kept blowing off my head as we tried to shoot those lines over to the *Mercer*. At one point, my head felt so numb I rubbed my hand over it and felt something. It was a big clump of ice, and when I pulled on it, a big patch of my hair came with it. But it was so cold I didn't even feel it."

As the lines fell short of their target, Captain Naab and his crew began a dangerous dance of positioning the cutter nearer to the bow of the *Mercer*. As the cutter maneuvered closer, however, Naab realized that the *Mercer*'s bow was surging so wildly that both vessels could collide, killing them all. The captain decided to edge away, hoping the storm would soon subside a bit before trying another rescue. For the next five and a half hours, the *Yakutat* stood by the bow of the *Mercer*, keeping a close watch for any sign of change.

~

While the *Yakutat* had made it to the scene of what it hoped would be a rescue, the 36-foot motor lifeboat skippered by Ralph Ormsby, which had left Nantucket at noon, was having no such luck. "We couldn't see anything," said Ormsby. "There were snow squalls, and the seas were tremendous."

When night fell, their orders changed once again, and they were told to seek safety. Ormsby steered his vessel and its frozen crew to the Pollock Rip Lightship. He was entering some of the most treacherous waters on the East Coast, the shifting labyrinth of shoals between Nantucket and the elbow of Cape Cod. The tides play havoc in the shallows here, creating rip currents of churning, sand-filled seas that can be frightening even on calm days. And now with monstrous waves, wind, and current colliding, Ormsby's small lifeboat was tossed about like so much flotsam. Should the boat capsize amid the breakers at the rip, he and his crew would be dead within minutes.

Somehow Ormsby navigated through the maze of shoals and pulled up alongside the lightship. Crewmember Alfred Roy stood on the bow of the lifeboat and attempted to throw a line with a weight at the end to the crew on the lightship. Just as Roy made the throw, the 36-footer was hit by a wave, and Roy went airborne, hitting his face against the oak planks of the bow. Ormsby tried to steady the wallowing vessel while Roy got back on his feet and hurled the line once again. This time, the lightship crew grabbed the other end, and the lifeboat was secured against the larger vessel. The men climbed aboard, where Roy had the gash above his eye attended to.

The second 36-footer sent out earlier that day, skippered by Donald Bangs, was having an equally harrowing mission. Bangs and his crew almost didn't survive the first few minutes of their journey, because when they rounded Monomoy Point, they were assaulted by a huge breaking sea. The skipper thought that if he tried to maneuver the boat over the waves, his vessel stood a good chance of having its bow go straight up and then over the stern, capsizing the lifeboat. He only had a minute to make a decision, but he gunned the engine and forced his tiny craft to punch *through* the waves. When he and his men came out the other side, they were completely airborne and then, free-falling, slammed into the trough below.

So far his mission had been one not only of danger but of frustration as well. He and his crew were originally sent to aid the *Mercer*. When they reached Pollock Rip Lightship, however, they were told to turn around and head back toward Chatham because the two halves of the *Pendleton* had been spotted there.

Donald Bangs was a quiet, even-tempered man, but even he must have voiced his frustration at spending the last couple of hours fighting the seas toward the *Mercer*, only to be told they needed to head to a new location. Like Ormsby and crew, the men on Bangs's boat had already suffered greatly. The open cockpit had no heat, and the men were repeatedly soaked by breaking seas and foam sheared from the crest of waves. Snow and sleet still fell, and the crew's ears, fingers, and toes were numb from the cold. Water had filled the men's boots, but the motion of the boat was so violent they couldn't even empty them.

At one point in the journey, one of the crewmen shouted to their skipper, "Are we going to make it?" Bangs, focusing on the next wave, shouted back, "How the hell do I know? I've never seen anything like this!"

Bangs finally saw the *Pendleton*'s bow section come into view, eerily riding the seas with its forward end pointed upward into the dark night. The superstructure and the bridge at the front end of the broken vessel were awash with churning seas. The icy slope of the deck from that end to the tip of the bow was roughly 45 degrees, seemingly too steep for someone to climb.

The bow was listing to port, and Bangs slowly circled the hulk, looking for any signs of movement or the flicker of a flashlight. Blasting his signal horn at short intervals, he hoped someone would appear on deck. He tried holding his lifeboat in one place, just downwind of the hulk. His crew listened intently for the shouts of trapped sailors. But there was only the wind; the bow appeared deserted.

Where are the crewmen? Bangs wondered. *Were they swept off the ship? Did they take to the lifeboats?* There were no clues. The fractured bow appeared to be a ghost ship, wallowing in the heavy seas, ready to descend to the depths at any moment.

And so the freezing crew of Bangs, Ballerini, Haynes, and Ciccone turned their vessel toward Chatham, thinking they could help locate the *Pendleton*'s stern. They were more than halfway to the stern when their radio crackled. The captain of the cutter *McCulluch*, which had recently arrived on the scene, shouted that he was at the bow of the *Pendleton* and they had just seen a light flicker—there were survivors on board after all!

For the third time, Bangs set a new course, racing as best he could in 50- to 60-foot seas back to the bow. This time he moved even closer to the hulk, and as the wave crests carried his small vessel upward, he and his men were almost at eye level with the deck of the broken ship. That's when they saw a lone man on the starboard wing.

"We saw a man standing on the bridge," recalled Bangs. "He

was hollering at us, but we couldn't hear a word. We went in close and could see that he was standing on the wing of the bridge. The wind and waves were pitching the ship at tremendous degrees. We tried to get a line aboard, but had to give up. The man was then seen to jump or fall into the sea. He came to the surface floating about a boat length and a half from us. Just as we were about to fish him out of the water, the biggest sea of the night broke over our deck."

Recovering from the blow, the skipper used his searchlight to try to find the man in the tumultuous seas. In the beam of the light, Bangs spotted him yards away, floating motionless on his back. Then the sea simply engulfed him, and his fight for life was over. Bangs and his crew searched and circled throughout the night, but they never saw the man again. Incredibly, the four coast guard men stayed out searching for survivors for several more hours, spending a total of 22 hours in storm-tossed seas.

None of the other seven men known to be on the *Pendleton* bow, including Captain Fitzgerald, ever appeared at the railing, fired a flare, or flashed a light, and they were assumed to have been swept off the ship long before Bangs made his heroic attempt to rescue the man who jumped.

~

Aboard the bow of the *Mercer*, Captain Paetzel and his crew were becoming desperate. The front of the bow section was sticking completely out of the water, but the aft section of the hulk, where

Paetzel and crew were trapped in the unheated chart room, was sinking lower into the sea. Just before midnight, they decided to try to move from the chart room to the forecastle room located at the very tip of the bow, where they hoped to escape the rising water.

To do so, however, first meant somehow lowering themselves out of the chart room and onto the exposed deck, which was awash with spray, snow, and sometimes the sea itself. The door from the chart room to the deck was too close to the sinking end of the hulk, and the drop from a porthole to the deck was too great to risk jumping. And so the crew improvised, taking various signal flags and tying them together to create a line, which they dropped out the porthole on the forward side of the chart room. One by one, the men started out. First they lowered themselves down the signal flag line, then took the most harrowing footsteps of their lives as they headed forward on the upward-sloping, icy catwalk.

The ship pitched and rolled, and the men ran toward the forecastle as seething white water surged around their feet. Radio operator John O'Reilly—who had been transmitting to Len Whitmore earlier that morning—slipped, lost his footing, and was swept overboard, disappearing into the churning abyss. The other eight crewmembers made it safely to the forecastle. Captain Paetzel, who had been wearing his slippers when the tanker split, made the crossing barefoot.

Captain Naab on the *Yakutat* had seen the men run across the catwalk, and he knew the tanker crewmen were desperate enough to do anything. He decided he had better make another attempt to get them off. He maneuvered the cutter windward of the tanker. His men then tied several life rafts in a row, dropped them overboard, and let the wind carry them toward the tanker. Lights and lifejackets were attached to each of the rafts.

On the *Mercer*'s bow, the survivors watched the rafts come toward them. It was decision time, and what an awful decision it was. Each man had to make a choice in the next minute that might mean the difference between life and death. There was no one to give them guidance, assurance, or even the odds they faced, because no one on earth knew what would happen next.

Three crewmembers on board felt the rafts were their best chance of escaping the storm alive. They crawled to the side of the deck and, one by one, threw themselves overboard and down toward the rafts. All three missed their target. The shock of the freezing water made swimming nearly impossible, and although they tried to get to the rafts, they disappeared from view. Captain Naab watched in horror as the mountainous seas buried the men.

One of the tanker crewmen, Jerome Higgins, still on board the *Mercer*, saw how close the *Yakutat* was and made a fatal choice. He leaped over the rail, hit the water, and tried to swim to the cutter. In the howling darkness, the seas swept him away in a flash. Naab, not wanting to witness any more drowning, backed the cutter away to wait for dawn.

Later, Naab would say that watching the crewmen jump

from the ship and be taken by the sea was "the worst hour of my life."

There were only four men left on the fractured bow of the *Mercer*: Captain Paetzel, purser Edward Turner, third mate Vincent Guldin, and first mate Willard Fahrner. Huddling together for warmth, they sat in shock, not quite believing that five fellow crewmen were dead or dying alone in the freezing ocean.

Naab on the *Yakutat* felt helpless. "There was nothing more we could do, so the operation was abandoned until daylight. We just kept praying the hulk would stay up."

9

LOSING ALL HOPE: ON BOARD THE *PENDLETON* STERN

Adrift now for nearly 14 hours, the men aboard the stern of the *Pendleton* still had food, water, and heat, but they were running low on hope. The rescue attempt for the *Fort Mercer* was fully under way, but the *Pendleton* crew had yet to hear anything on the radio about their own plight. Chief engineer Ray Sybert had become de facto captain of the stern section, and he was scared. He tried to keep his composure and conceal his dread from his men.

The crew had obviously grown much closer during the time of their ordeal, but the tremendous strain was beginning to show on most everyone. Wallace Quirey wished he still had his Bible with him. He could hear his mother's soft voice echoing in his mind. "Keep it with you always," she had told him. "It will protect you."

One crewmember, however, maintained his confidence. George Myers had spent much of the day shooting off flares, hoping someone onshore would see them. Myers was a native of Avella, Pennsylvania, a coal-mining town less than an hour from Pittsburgh. He served as an oiler and part-time cook and no doubt enjoyed the taste of the food he helped to prepare. He weighed well over 300 pounds and was known affectionately as Tiny by the crew. He was such an affable fellow that one crewmember, 23-year-old Rollo Kennison of Kalamazoo, Michigan, had even gushed that Tiny Myers was "the greatest man on earth." Kennison had watched his large friend lift spirits among the crew for much of the day, and now he was watching Myers point his flare gun up toward the dark, swirling winds. Myers shot off another flare and handed the gun to Kennison. "Keep that, kid," he said with a smile. "I want it as a souvenir when we get to shore."

~

Eighteen-year-old Charles Bridges periodically went out on deck, hoping to see a rescue boat approaching. One of these forays nearly cost him his life. "The spray had frozen on the decks, and when a big swell hit the ship, I lost my footing and started sliding across the deck. There was no way I could stop myself. I could see that my last chance was to grab the ship's railing and that, if I didn't, I'd be swept right under it and overboard. Luckily I got a hold of it. Had I slid toward the front, I would have gone right overboard where the ship had cracked."

Bridges said his spirits were at their lowest about mid-afternoon. "That's when we hit a shoal and it stopped the drifting. Every time a wave slammed the ship, it pushed us over another inch. Soon the ship had a bad list, and men were talking about launching the lifeboats. A big discussion ensued about taking to the lifeboats. I said, 'You're crazy if you think I'm going in one of those. As long as this ship floats, I'm staying right here.' I knew that if we got in the lifeboats, we probably couldn't even get away from the ship. The waves would have crushed us against the hull. And even if the lifeboat got out from under the ship, where was the coast? No one knew how far it was, and no one knew if the coast would even offer us a place to wash up. Even though the deck kept sloping, no one ever did launch one of the boats."

The full impact of the storm was now reaching the public as Monday evening newspapers reported on the ongoing ocean rescues as well as the onshore calamities. On the *Boston Globe*'s front page, a report stated that the storm had killed 15 people from New England in various accidents, mostly on the snow-covered roads or from heart attacks while shoveling. Over 1,000 motorists had been stranded in their cars on the Maine Turnpike since the storm first hit one night earlier.

The storm dumped over two feet of snow in central Maine,

and the *Boston Globe* reported 20,000 MAROONED IN 3 MAINE TOWNS, explaining that the towns of Rumford, Andover, and Mexico were cut off from the outside world by giant snowdrifts. Food and fuel were running low, and "volunteers are being sought to reinforce the already doubled snow crews working with all available equipment at hand trying to break through 10- to 12-foot drifts."

By the next edition of the newspaper, the death toll on land had more than doubled. The *Globe* reported, "New England was on its knees today after the worst snowstorm in years. The gale-driven northeaster left in its wake millions of dollars worth of damage and at least 33 deaths."

There were lucky people, however, as well as the unlucky. In Bar Harbor, Maine, three days after the storm, police were using long poles to poke through snowbanks, hoping to find a car that had been seen skidding off the road. While probing a particularly deep drift by the side of Route 3, police chief Howard Mac-Farland thought he heard a muffled yell from the snowy depths. MacFarland started clawing and digging the hard-packed snow away until he saw a car below him. He continued digging until he reached the driver-side door. Then, according to the *Boston Herald*, out stepped 20-year-old George Delaney, "stiff-jointed and blinking but otherwise apparently in good shape." Delaney had been entombed for more than two full days.

For Bernie and his crew, the storm's challenge wasn't snow but wind-driven waves as big as two-story houses. This blizzard was dangerous on land—but absolutely deadly at sea.

10

ALL BUT ONE:
THE RESCUE OF THE
PENDLETON STERN

On board Bernie Webber's lifeboat, the engine was dead, and the crew would be too if they couldn't get it restarted soon. The sturdy vessel had one flaw: the engine stalled if the boat rolled too much while it was under way. Andy Fitzgerald began carefully making his way from the bow to the engine compartment. The *CG 36500* continued to pitch and rear violently as Fitzgerald tried to keep a firm grip on the rails.

He got to the engine room and crawled into the small space, made even smaller by the wet, heavy clothes he had on. Once inside the compartment, another heavy wave slammed into the lifeboat, bouncing Fitzgerald around the engine room. Andy cried out as he was thrown like a rag doll against the hot engine. Despite suffering burns, bruises, and scrapes, he somehow managed to control the pain as he held down the priming lever and waited for the gasoline to begin flowing to the engine again. Andy restarted the 90-horsepower motor.

As the motor kicked back to life, Bernie Webber noticed a change in the seas. The waves were more monstrous now, but they were also spread farther apart. This told him that he and his crew had defied the odds. They had made it over Chatham Bar.

In many ways, however, their nightmare had only just begun. They were outside the bar, but Bernie had no idea of their exact location. He pushed the throttle down and headed deeper into the teeth of the storm. *If only I can make it to the Pollock Rip Lightship, I think we'll be okay*, he told himself. He had no compass, and the radio was so tied up with traffic that it was utterly useless to him now.

It was a dance of giants as the 60- to 70-foot waves rose and fell. The men's senses were heightened; they were assaulted by roaring wind when their boat rode up to the top of waves, then enveloped in an eerie quiet as they plunged down into the valleys. All were soaked from the bone-chilling ocean, but so much adrenaline was coursing through them that they hardly noticed. Each time the boat plunged into a trough, icy spray and foam slapped them in the face, and Webber fought the wheel to prevent the boat from broaching. They kept their knees bent, trying to anticipate the impact of each oncoming wave. While Webber clung to the wheel, Livesey, Fitz, and Maske kept a vise-like grip on the rails, believing if they were hurled out of the boat, they would likely never be found.

The storm grew stronger as they ventured farther out to sea, where the cauldron of wind and snow intensified even more. Webber's only option was to ride the waves like a thunderous roller coaster. He let the *CG 36500*'s engine idle as they climbed slowly and steadily up toward the wave's curled, frothing peak. Bernie gunned the engine to get them over the top of the wave, and they all held on as the lifeboat raced down the other side.

Like the men aboard the stern section of the *Pendleton*, the crew of the *CG 36500* also prayed this would not be their last night on earth. Although Webber wouldn't admit it to his men, his hope was fading. Again, he thought of Miriam sick in bed at home. Who would be the one to tell her that her husband was not ever to return? Bernie tried to shake the image and refocused his attention on the angry seas ahead. He peered through the broken glass of the windshield and felt his heart jump. Webber could see a mysterious dark shape rising menacingly out of the surf. He slowed the lifeboat almost to a stop. *There's something there*, he told himself.

"Andy! Go to the bow and turn on the searchlight!" Webber hollered. Fitzgerald moved carefully toward the forward cabin and flicked on the searchlight switch. A small beam of light was cast, illuminating the huge object that was now less than 50 feet away. Had Webber gone any farther, he would have collided with it. The steel hulk was dark and ominous, with no apparent signs of life.

My God, we're too late, Bernie thought. *It's a ghost ship.*

Raymond Sybert fought back his darkest thoughts as he and 32 other men sat helplessly inside the stern section of the *Pendleton*. There was nothing left for the men to do but ride out the storm and wait for help to arrive. *If it arrived.* Just then, the man on watch noticed something—a small light, headed their way.

Frank Fauteux and Charles Bridges also saw the light. "It was the most glorious sight," said Fauteux, "this single light bobbing up and down in the rolling seas. No one cheered. We just watched, spellbound." Bridges recalled that the light looked no bigger than a pinprick in the inky blackness, mesmerizing as it went up and over the huge seas, slowly inching closer.

~

Bernie Webber motored the *CG 36500* in for a better look as Andy Fitzgerald continued to run the searchlight up and across the wide girth of the tanker. The beam of light flashed on the name *Pendleton* painted high up along the side of the hulk. The giant ship looked enormous and indestructible. *How could it have split in two?* Webber thought as he maneuvered his tiny lifeboat down the portside of the stern.

A sense of guilt came over Bernie Webber as he came to realize that he had jeopardized the lives of his men for a lost cause. *This is a useless trip. The seamen aboard the* Pendleton *didn't have a chance,* Bernie thought. *And now my men have little chance of returning home alive.*

An eerie silence hung over the ship as the wide-eyed lifeboat crew inspected the wreckage. The silence was broken by eerie groaning sounds as they arrived at the gaping hole that was once connected to the bow. The men looked inside the intestines of the ship with its shredded compartments and its loose steel beams and plates swaying back and forth in the frothing surf. Webber steered away from the giant tunnel leading to the bowels of the ship and guided the lifeboat around the stern, where the crew was startled by something else now. A string of lights glowed high up on the ship's decks—the fractured stern had not lost power after all. In the twinkle of the lights, they could also see a small figure! A man was waving his arms wildly!

They had not come for nothing.

But how would they get this man off the high deck? The survivor would have to jump, and there was a strong possibility he would be engulfed by the waves. As the *CG 36500* crew contemplated the next course of action, the man on the high decks disappeared. *Where did he go?* Bernie asked himself.

Suddenly, the figure returned, and this time he was not alone. Three additional men were with him, then four or five more appeared, and new figures kept coming. Within a minute's time, more than two dozen survivors in orange life jackets lined the rails! All of them looked directly down at the

diminutive lifeboat trying to maintain position in the tumultuous seas.

Fred Brown and Tiny Myers were standing side by side on
the rail. Tiny turned to Fred and, pulling his wallet out of his
trousers, said, "Take my wallet. I don't think I'll get through
this one." Fred was taken aback by the comment but retorted,
"You've got just as good a chance as I have." Brown took the
wallet and stuck it right back in Tiny's hip pocket.

Bernie, looking at the shadowy figures above, was first over-
joyed at seeing so many sailors alive, but he quickly came to a
frightening realization. It might be impossible to fit all those
men on the 36-foot lifeboat. The responsibility hit Webber like
a tidal wave. *How are we going to save all these men? If I fail, what a
tragedy this will be.*

Still gazing up at the deck, Bernie saw a rope ladder with
wooden steps, called a Jacob's ladder, drop over the side of the
Pendleton. And in the next instant, the stranded seamen started
coming down the ladder as fast as they could.

The first man down the ladder jumped and landed with a
loud crash on the bow of the lifeboat. The others clung tightly to
the rope as it swayed dangerously outward while the *Pendleton*
rocked in the seas. Their screams echoed over the swirling
winds as they slammed back against the hull when the ship rolled
in the opposite direction.

Bernie drove the lifeboat in toward the hull, trying to time
the maneuver just right so each survivor would land on the boat
and not in the icy water. With the rolling seas, this proved to

be an impossible task. Some of the survivors leaped toward the lifeboat only to find themselves plunging into the frigid swells below. The *CG 36500* was fitted with a safety line wrapped around the shell of the boat, and the soaked seamen eventually found their way to the surface and held on to the rope for dear life.

Fitzgerald, Maske, and Livesey took hold of the waterlogged men and hoisted them aboard. The crew scrambled quickly for fear the survivors would be swept under the bow of the lifeboat. All the while, Webber kept a steady hand on the wheel, making passes each time a desperate man jumped from the Jacob's ladder. Once the survivors were safely on board, Andy, Ervin, and Richard led them down to the forward cabin and herded them inside, but that small space was filling up quickly. With the added weight, the *CG 36500* was now taking on a lot of water, and as captain of the boat, Bernie had to make a life-and-death decision. *Do we stop now and try to get the men we have safely back to shore? Or do we go for broke?* Webber decided that no man would be left behind. "We would all live, or we would all die," he said later.

While the rescue was unfolding, the stern section of the *Pendleton* rolled deeply and increased its list to port, scraping mightily against the ocean floor. The lifeboat crew continued to take survivors aboard, squeezing them in anywhere they could. The engine compartment was now overflowing with human cargo, as was the area around the wheelman's shelter. Bernie fought for elbow room as he continued to make passes along the stricken tanker. He had to time his maneuvers perfectly, or the waves would send the lifeboat surging into the tanker hull and they'd all be swallowed by the sea.

~

Thirty-one survivors were now on board a vessel designed to carry only 12 men. Two men were still on the tanker's deck: Raymond Sybert, who as de facto captain of the stern would be the last man off, and Tiny Myers. Fitzgerald kept the searchlight on the beefy man as he made his way slowly down the Jacob's ladder. Myers was shirtless now, having given much of his own clothing to warm up other members of the *Pendleton* crew. The swells surrounding the ship had become even more violent at this point, making it a greater challenge for Bernie to steer the lifeboat. *Just a couple more, and we can get the hell outta here*, he thought.

Myers had made it halfway down the ladder when he suddenly slipped and fell into the ocean. He resurfaced seconds later, and the lifeboat crew tried frantically to pull him on board. "Come this way!" Andy yelled. Myers drifted over to the inboard side of the lifeboat and grabbed hold of the line. Richard Livesey then leaned far over the side of the vessel and reached for Myers's hand. The move nearly cost Livesey his life. Myers was so heavy and strong that he began to pull Richard down into the water. Ervin and Andy rushed over to help, grabbing hold of Livesey by the legs and waist to prevent him from being pulled overboard.

As they tried in vain to hoist Myers into the boat, the large man was swallowed by an even larger wave and disappeared from sight. A collective gasp of horror could be heard on the lifeboat as the survivors watched their friend be consumed by the sea. Bernie put the lifeboat in reverse and maneuvered away from the side of the ship. The *CG 36500* came around in a circle as Andy kept the spotlight shining on the cresting waves. They finally caught sight of Myers in the darkness.

Due to the angle of the stern, the three propeller blades were now sticking out of the water. The seas were picking up, and Webber knew that he'd have only one chance to save this man. He steered the bow of the lifeboat toward Myers and then eased slowly ahead. At that moment, Webber and crew felt the back of the boat rise up as a huge wave lifted the *CG 36500* and threw it against the ship. The lifeboat was now out of control and rushing toward Myers. Webber could see the panicked look in the man's eyes. Ervin Maske reached out and managed to grab hold of the man once more, but the lifeboat was careering toward the ship. A second later, they felt the sudden impact of a collision as the lifeboat slammed into the tanker, trapping Tiny Myers between them.

THIRTY-SIX MEN
IN A 36-FOOT BOAT

Webber had tried desperately to avoid Tiny Myers as the lifeboat lurched forward. He even tried throwing the *CG 36500* in reverse, but that only stalled the engine once more. Ervin Maske was the last man to get ahold of Myers, and he paid a price for it. Maske's hands had been crushed in the collision, and he could feel the blood pumping in his fingertips, which were now beginning to swell. There would be no way to recover the body now. Webber tried to put the thought out of his mind. He successfully maneuvered the boat back to the ladder, rescuing the last man down, Raymond Sybert.

Andy Fitzgerald crawled back into the engine compartment in hopes of getting the motor going again. The lifeboat took another violent punch from a wave, throwing Andy back on top of the engine at the moment it restarted. Webber heard his comrade scream as the spark plugs burned his back. Bernie was about to send another crewmember into the compartment when Fitzgerald suddenly dragged himself out. Andy could feel the welts growing on his back, but otherwise he was okay. Webber and crew had conquered Chatham Bar, and getting the survivors off the *Pendleton*'s stern was a huge accomplishment, but making it safely back to shore would have its own set of perils.

Drifting in the darkness and with no compass to guide them, Webber still had no idea exactly where they were. Also, he didn't know where the other coast guard boats were, but he understood that his vessel must have remained somewhere off Chatham or maybe somewhere to the south of Monomoy Island. *If I can just put the sea behind me and jog along, we'll end up in Nantucket Sound and eventually on the shallow water somewhere on Cape Cod,* he tried to convince himself. Bernie then relayed his plans to the rest of the men on board.

"If the boat all of a sudden stops, hit the beach," he commanded. "Don't waste any time asking questions. Get off and help those who are hurt. Just get off as fast as you can!"

Webber felt that if he could get the boat's bow as close as possible to the storm-tossed beach and keep the engine going, the men would have the precious few moments they would need to get safely ashore. The survivors understood the plan perfectly. "We're with you, coxswain!" a shout came out. It was followed by a loud cheer from the *Pendleton* crew.

At least one member of the lifeboat crew was not so optimistic, however. "The worst time for me was when we were going back in," Richard Livesey recalled. His arms were pinned by the crush of men standing in the well deck in front of the broken windshield. They were now back in gigantic seas, without the protection that had been provided by the sheer mass of the *Pendleton* stern. The *CG 36500* was weighed down by its human cargo as powerful waves continued to crash over its crowded deck. Livesey and the others held their breath as each wave hit, engulfing them in a torrent of ice-cold water. *When will this end?* Livesey wondered. It felt like an eternity. The lifeboat was riding so low it felt like they were all traveling in a submarine. *If she doesn't come up a bit more, I'm gonna drown right here in the boat,* Livesey thought.

Webber tried the radio once more and was surprised to get through to the Chatham Lifeboat Station. Station commander Cluff seemed even more surprised to hear from him. Webber informed Cluff that they had 32 men from the *Pendleton* aboard and that they were now trying to make it back, despite having no navigational tools to assist them. The captain of one of the rescue cutters called in and directed Webber to turn around and proceed out to sea toward his location, thinking this would be safer than recrossing Chatham Bar. Bernie heard more squawking over the radio and yet more ideas on how better to pull off this already improbable rescue. But Webber and crew had made up their minds. They were headed to shore. Bernie put the radio down and returned his attention to the challenge in front of him. There was no talking aboard the lifeboat while Bernie attacked the seas ahead.

As the *CG 36500* motored on, the seas began to change. The waves were not as heavy, nor were they spread as far apart, as they had been. The boat moved through shallower waters now. By no means were they out of danger, however. They still had Chatham Bar to navigate. Webber was weighing his options when he noticed what appeared to be a flashing red light in the distance. Could it be a buoy? Could it be the aircraft warning signal from high atop the RCA radio station towers? Bernie rubbed his tired, salt-burned eyes. At one moment, the light seemed to be well over their heads; at another, it appeared to be well below the lifeboat.

As they continued on, the blinking red light became clearer. The crew realized it was coming from atop the buoy inside Chatham Bar, leading to the entrance into Old Harbor. Bernie looked at the blinking light once more and then shifted his gaze to the stormy skies above. In his heart, he knew that God was bringing them home.

PANDEMONIUM
IN CHATHAM

The *CG 36500* was now on a course that would return its crew and the 32 survivors of the *Pendleton* to the Chatham Fish Pier. They still had to make it over Chatham Bar, where the boat had nearly been sunk hours earlier. This time the vessel would be going with the seas, and as they approached the bar, the crew noticed the crashing surf didn't seem to be as loud as it had been before. Their weak spotlight shined on the breakers, yet they too seemed smaller.

Webber gave the boat a little throttle, punched its nose through the foam, and they were over the bar. He then radioed the Chatham Lifeboat Station and told the operator his position. Stunned that they had actually made it back to Old Harbor, the

operator immediately sent a dispatch to the other coast guard
vessels:

CG 36500 HAS 32 MEN ABOARD FROM
THE STERN SECTION. ALL EXCEPT ONE
MAN WHO IS ON THE WATER THAT THEY
CANNOT GET. NO OTHER MEN ARE
MISSING THAT THEY KNOW OF. THERE
SHOULD BE ABOUT SIX MEN ON THE BOW
SECTION. . . .

An avalanche of instructions followed as the operator tried to
guide Webber up the harbor. But Bernie didn't need instructions. "I was very familiar with Old Harbor and had been up
and down it many times," he later wrote in his memoir. "I knew
where the shoal spots were and when the turns had to be made.
I was in no mood to listen to the chatter on the radio."

News of the rescue sparked more than chatter on the Fish
Pier, where Chatham residents had been waiting anxiously for
word. Thunderous applause rippled across the pier as townspeople hugged and cried while waiting for sight of the boat.

Tears were also being shed on board the *CG 36500*. Bernie
heard crying from the men stuffed in the lifeboat's tiny forward
compartment. Despite calmer waters and what must have been
intense feelings of claustrophobia, the survivors remained holed
up in the cabin, refusing to come out until they had reached port.

The small but sturdy lifeboat was now in sight, and the throngs of people gathered at the Fish Pier struggled for a closer look. Photographer Dick Kelsey positioned his big camera and began photographing what would become some of the most indelible images in Cape Cod history. Kelsey captured the battered vessel on film as it came in, rubbing against the wooden pylons. He could see the faces of the frightened but thankful men peering through the boat's shattered windshield and out of every porthole.

At that moment, Bernie gazed up at the Fish Pier and saw well over a hundred local residents. They were the men, women, and children of Chatham, and all appeared to be reaching out their hands to grab the boat's lines to help. The Ryder children stood close to their father, David, a longtime Chatham fisherman who knew Bernie well, knew that he was a more-than-competent coast guardsman. Yet even he had not given Webber and his crew much of a chance that night. "There was great concern that the crew wouldn't make it," Ryder recalled afterward. "There's no question he [Bernie] was a good man and had experience on the Bar, but none of us had ever seen a storm like this." Like most people huddled on the pier that night, Ryder couldn't believe his eyes when he saw the small lifeboat making its way home. "She was coming in very low, and I was amazed at how many people came pouring out of her."

Once the *CG 36500* was safely tied up to the pier, townspeople aided the shaken survivors off the boat. The vessel had been so weighed down that Richard Livesey felt it rise each

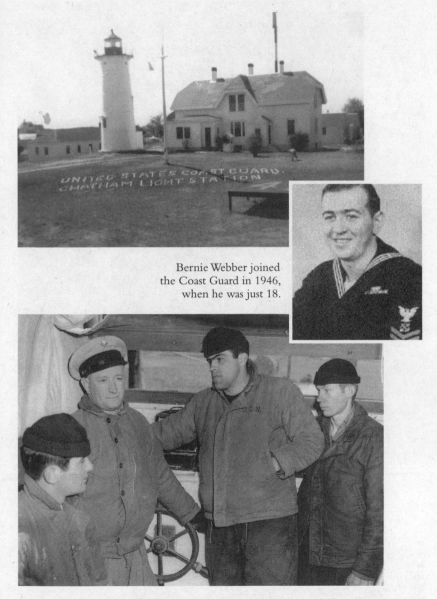

Coast Guard Chatham Lifeboat Station overlooks the waters off Cape Cod. This is where Bernie Webber was stationed. [Courtesy Mel Guthro]

Bernie Webber joined the Coast Guard in 1946, when he was just 18.

Skipper Donald Bangs (in the light-colored hat) and his crew manned the first lifeboat sent from Chatham. From left to right: Antonio Ballerini, Donald Bangs, Richard Ciccone, and Emory Haynes.

The *CG 36500* is the rescue boat Bernie and crew took into the storm.

The crew of the *CG 36500* spent hours battling the storm, searching for survivors. From left to right: Bernie Webber, Richard Livesey, and Andy Fitzgerald (Ervin Maske not pictured). [Kelsey Photo]

The Coast Guard cutter *Yakutat*.

The bow section of the *Pendleton* after it split in half.

Crewmembers of the *Yakutat* pull a life raft with two survivors back to the cutter.

The lifeboat from the *Yakutat* returns with two survivors from the sinking *Fort Mercer* bow. Captain Paetzel is on board.

A survivor from the *Fort Mercer* in a life raft.

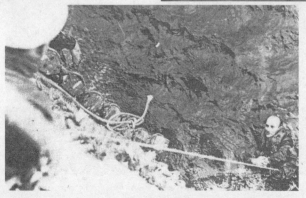

The last survivor from the *Fort Mercer* bow is hauled up.

The *Fort Mercer*'s bow capsizes just minutes after the last two men jumped into a raft.

The last photo of the *Fort Mercer*'s bow before it sank.

The *Fort Mercer* stern section after it split in half.

The *Eastwind* arrives at the *Fort Mercer*'s stern section.

A life raft with one survivor in it is pulled to the *Eastwind* from the tanker.

The crew of the *CG 36500* returns to Chatham pier as onlookers wait anxiously.
[Kelsey Photo]

The men of the *CG 36500*, exhausted but grateful to be safely back on dry land.
From left to right: Bernie Webber, Andy Fitzgerald, Richard Livesey, Ervin Maske.
[Kelsey Photo]

Captain John Joseph of the *Acushnet* is thanked
by one of the survivors he rescued.

Volunteers repaired the *CG 36500*,
and today it floats at Rock Harbor
in Orleans, Massachusetts.

The *Pendleton* stern rescue made the
headlines of the *Boston Daily Globe*.
Bernie and his crew were called heroes
in newspapers across the country.

Andy and Gloria Fitzgerald with their granddaughter Kelly Ann Fitzgerald
aboard the *CG 36500* in 2010.

time a man got off. An exhausted Bernie Webber stood quietly at the vessel's stern, his elbow resting on top of the cockpit, his forearm supporting his head. His mind was filled with the terrifying images of the past several hours and the bravery of his crew. He thought about Tiny Myers and the look in the doomed man's eyes just seconds before he was killed. He thought about the 32 survivors on board. And he thought about Miriam, and how he would be returning to her after all. His tired fingers began to tremble, and soon his whole body was shaking. Webber cried openly and thanked God for guiding them home. Dick Kelsey watched in silence and realized how Webber's private moment could symbolize the ordeal each man had gone through. "It was quite a while before he left," Kelsey said later. "All of the men had gone off by then, but he just stood there in a daze. What a wonderful thing he'd done."

The survivors were now being crammed into automobiles for the ride to the Chatham Lifeboat Station. Thirty-four-year-old Joe Nickerson, a lifelong Chatham resident, drove two of the men in his Ford sedan. "I drove one fella," Nickerson remembered. "He told me that he was on the forward section of the ship when it split in two. He said that he saved himself by jumping over a huge crack back to the stern. If he hadn't done that, he'd have been swept away with the bow." However, the *Pendleton* survivors refused to call their skipper and eight others *missing*. The men were still holding on to the belief that their comrades would be found alive.

The survivors were whisked to the station, where they were

met by local physician Dr. Carroll Keene. He knew right away that many of the men were in a state of shock. "One of the fellows I drove down simply collapsed once we got inside the station," Joe Nickerson recalled. "Then it was like dominoes, another guy fell, and then another. We had eight guys laid out on the floor completely unconscious." Red Cross leader Leroy Anderson and his unit assisted Dr. Keene. Tailor Ben Shufro, manager of Puritan Clothing on Main Street in Chatham, had a tape measure around his neck and was fitting those survivors who remained on their feet for new clothes that he had donated. Reverend Steve Smith of the United Methodist Church was also on hand to offer prayers for the survivors. The reverend's presence was especially comforting to Wallace Quirey. The seaman approached the minister and told him that he had lost his Bible during the mad scramble on board the ship. Reverend Smith nodded and gave Quirey his own copy of the Holy Book.

John Stello, Bernie Webber's friend and neighbor, called Webber's home and broke the news to Miriam, who was still in bed with the flu. Her husband was being hailed as a hero, and Stello told her why.

~

Bushy-browed WOCB newsman Ed Semprini had survived the grueling drive down snow-covered Route 28. The bad weather had not let up during the 21-mile trek from Hyannis to Chatham.

Semprini arrived at the Chatham Lifeboat Station, where he met up with his engineer Wes Stidstone. Both men were wired for sound when the *Pendleton* survivors came dragging in. Semprini knew that he didn't have much time. He had to get the interviews done quickly so that they could drive back to the radio station in Yarmouth and broadcast live. He put his microphone in nearly every tired man's face as they warmed up on coffee and doughnuts. The accents befuddled the veteran newsman, who was himself still learning to understand how Cape Codders spoke. "One survivor from Louisiana asked me if his family could hear him speaking live." Semprini explained that the interviews would later be aired coast-to-coast on the Mutual News Network. Every survivor Semprini interviewed that night could not say enough about Bernie Webber and his crew. "They called it a miracle," Semprini remembered with a smile.

Webber, meanwhile, had gone upstairs to his bunk at the Chatham Lifeboat Station, still shaken by the long hours spent riding the biggest waves in the worst storm of his life. He bent down and kicked off his overshoes. He then called Miriam. "I'm fine, and I'll be in touch with you tomorrow," he said. *A cup of mud and a doughnut wouldn't feel half bad right now*, he thought. Webber made his way down to the galley, where he met Andy, Richard, and Ervin. They all nodded toward one another. No one had to say a word. They would leave that to Daniel Cluff, who offered words of congratulations and admitted that he doubted he'd see any of them alive again. Ed Semprini had been searching for Bernie and finally spotted him coming out of the galley. Webber had been called the true hero of the rescue, and the newsman understood why. Bernie answered a few questions as coherently as possible. He had finished his cup of coffee and devoured his doughnut, and now all he wanted was sleep. He returned to his bunk and collapsed. Webber was safe now, but as he drifted off to sleep, he thought only about those still fighting the storm at sea.

PART II

THE *MERCER*'S BOW
CAPSIZES

As Chatham celebrated the rescue of the sailors from the *Pendleton*'s stern, the survivors still on board the *Fort Mercer*'s drifting bow huddled together for warmth. They had watched several of their crewmates fall to their deaths, and now, in the darkness, all they could do was wait for dawn and hope that the cutter *Yakutat*, which was standing by, would somehow get them off before they went down with the ship.

Captain Naab had spent a sleepless night on the *Yakutat*, staring at the huge black hulk of the *Mercer* and praying it would stay afloat until dawn. And so when the captain saw the first hint of light to the east, he was relieved. He was also thankful that the snow and sleet had let up. The wind was still howling, but the seas seemed to have eased a bit, dropping from the

50- and 60-foot range to about 40 feet. Now Naab went over his options. After what had transpired the preceding night, he did not want to send over more life rafts. He was afraid that if the survivors fell into the frigid ocean, they simply would not have the strength or the dexterity to stay afloat or climb into the rafts. Naab knew that the only way the men could be saved was if some of his own crewmen were waiting for them. He then made a fateful decision. The cutter's 26-foot lifeboat would be launched with a crew of five. It was a gamble to be sure; now Naab had to worry not only about the survival of the tanker's crewmen but about his own men who might be lost as well.

The skipper also feared that the men left on the *Mercer's* bow might, upon seeing a lifeboat coming their way, jump too soon. He picked up a loudspeaker and shouted to the survivors that he was sending over a lifeboat and that the lifeboat crew would signal to them when it was time to jump. He told the survivors that when the time came, they should jump into the ocean next to the lifeboat, and his men would pull them up. Naab knew that if this rescue failed, he would be second-guessed and the deaths of the men would forever haunt him. But, looking out at the bow, he thought the half ship was in danger of capsizing at any time. He could not afford to wait a moment longer.

The lifeboat was referred to as a "Monomoy surfboat" because it was designed with a high bow for the big surf that crashed into Monomoy Island, just off Chatham. But the 40-foot seas swirling around the *Yakutat* might be more than the wooden lifeboat was capable of handling. If the lifeboat capsized, the crew on board would have fewer than ten minutes of consciousness before hypothermia snuffed them out.

Ensign William Kiely, of Long Branch, New Jersey, was selected to lead the daring rescue, and he would be joined by Gil Carmichael, Paul Black, Edward Mason Jr., and Walter Terwilliger. One of the most dangerous parts of the mission would be at the very beginning: the lifeboat had to clear away from the *Yakutat* before waves slammed her back into the cutter and swamped her.

Carmichael later remembered how he and his fellow crewmen nervously boarded the lifeboat, and the men on board the cutter began lowering them with block, tackle, and winch. "The seas were so rough that the launch swung away from the ship and then slammed back into it. We didn't realize it at the time, but I think that cracked the wooden side of the boat. When we set down on the water, that's when I fully realized how small our launch was compared to the seas, and I had my doubts whether or not I'd ever get on the cutter alive again."

The four coasties navigated the lifeboat through the giant swells and pulled up alongside the massive steel hull of the *Mercer*, careful not to get too close.

Inside the broken bow of the *Mercer*, an argument broke out about who would jump first. Captain Paetzel said he wanted to be the last to leave, but his men felt that because of the deteriorating condition of his feet and the weakness he was showing from hypothermia, he should be the first to go. None of the men knew if the tiny lifeboat would be able to handle all four of them, nor did they know if the men in the launch were really going to be able to pluck them out of the seas. But they all felt it was a chance they'd have to take: if they stayed on board and the ship capsized, that would be the end. The crewmen told Captain Paetzel that if he didn't jump first, they'd throw him over.

The *Mercer* men—Paetzel, Turner, Guldin, and Fahrner—now moved out on the heaving deck, peering down at the lifeboat bobbing wildly in the waves below. It would be a long drop to the water. If they jumped into the trough of a wave, it would be approximately a 60-foot free fall, but if they sprang into a wave top, it would be only about 20 feet.

Ensign Kiely looked up at Captain Paetzel and signaled him to jump. Paetzel had reluctantly agreed to go first, but now he must have wondered if he was jumping to his death. The lifeboat below looked like a child's toy, insignificant against the towering seas.

Paetzel waited for a wave crest to rise up toward him. Then he jumped. He hit the water several feet from the lifeboat, first plunging completely underwater before the buoyancy of his life-jacket brought him back to the surface. The shock took his breath away and sent pain screaming through his body. He bobbed in the life-robbing seas, his arms already weak and growing numb. Precious seconds went by as he watched the lifeboat crew struggle to turn the boat toward him.

Kiely and crew did their best to maneuver the pitching lifeboat alongside the captain without hitting him. A minute had passed since the captain landed in the ocean, and they could see he was coughing up seawater. When they were an arm's length away, one of the coasties grabbed Paetzel's lifejacket, pulling him toward the boat. The waterlogged clothing on the captain doubled his weight, and at least three of the coast guardsmen used their combined strength to yank him on board.

During this time, Kiely did his best to keep the lifeboat clear of the ship's steel hull. Now that the captain was safely on board, he turned the boat and came around again to a position below the three remaining crewmembers. It was Turner's time to leap, and the purser waited on the sloping ship's deck for Kiely's signal. He had seen the difficulty the coasties had maneuvering to the captain, and he hoped they would be able to get to him without incident. Watching the little Monomoy surfboat below, he must have wondered how the men on board were managing to keep it upright in such large seas.

Kiely motioned for him to jump, and Turner did, trying to time his leap with the upward advance of a wave and clear the *Mercer*'s hull with room to spare. As Turner plunged into the seas, a wave lifted the lifeboat high in the air, and a following wave sent it flying toward him. There was only an instant to make a lunge for Turner, but the young coasties grabbed the purser as they swept by. As the men were trying to drag Turner aboard, the lifeboat slammed into the hull of the half tanker.

The jolt almost knocked the coast guardsmen out of the boat, but they kept their grip on Turner and hauled him up. The lifeboat, however, did not fare as well. Its wooden side was crushed, and water came cascading in over the broken gunnel, or rim. The added weight of the water, along with that of Paetzel and Turner, made the boat ride low, and Kiely had trouble controlling the vessel.

The lifeboat was sinking!

Kiely knew he'd have to abort the rescue or risk losing all six men on board the lifeboat. Captain Naab realized the same, and over the loudspeaker, he ordered Kiely to return. The young ensign, overwhelmed at having to leave men still on the hulk, had tears in his eyes, but he turned the tiny craft back toward the *Yakutat* and ever so slowly began navigating through the seas toward safety.

"I kept expecting our boat to capsize," said Carmichael. "We were very low in the water, and the seas were coming in the boat, entering over the sides and through cracks in the hull. The survivors lay on the bottom of the boat in the sloshing water, where they had collapsed."

When the lifeboat reached the cutter, hooks were lowered to secure the bow and stern. "We got the bow hook on without a problem," continued Carmichael. "But as I turned to get the swinging hook for the stern, it slammed into the side of my head, stunning me. Somehow we got that hook on our stern, and we were raised to the cutter's deck. That's when I fell unconscious. The next thing I remember, I woke up in my bunk."

Back on the *Mercer*'s bow, Guldin and Fahrner stood outside on the deck, relieved to see the lifeboat safely hoisted on board the cutter. But they also knew they had just lost their best chance of being rescued. The crushed lifeboat could not be used again, nor would Captain Naab risk another boat and crew, and these last two survivors wondered if the floating steel hulk they were standing on would be their coffin. There was nothing they could do now but wait.

~

On board the *Yakutat*, at approximately ten A.M., the radioman sent the following message to the Coast Guard Communications Center in Marshfield, Massachusetts:

```
TWO SURVIVORS, FREDERICK C. PAETZEL
(MASTER) AND EDWARD E. TURNER
(PURSER), RESCUED BY BOAT. WEATHER
CONDITIONS WORSENING. NOT ABLE TO
USE BOAT FOR REMAINING TWO MEN.
WILL ATTEMPT RESCUE BY SHOT LINE
AND RUBBER RAFT.
```

Captain Naab, realizing the wind had eased a bit from the prior day, reconsidered the option of sending over a life raft. He thought a messenger line could be successfully shot to the *Mercer*'s bow. The plan was to have a rubber life raft tied to the end of the messenger line and another line that would extend from the life raft back to the *Yakutat*. If all went well, the two remaining survivors would pull their end of the line and bring the raft toward them, securing their end to the tanker to keep the raft in place. Eyewitnesses differ in their accounts regarding what was supposed to transpire next. One scenario was to have a survivor jump off the tanker and swim to the raft, and once he got himself safely on board, the next man was to untie the messenger line from the tanker and fasten it around his waist. Then he too would leap off the tanker, and the first man would haul him to the life raft and help him aboard.

The second scenario was that the two survivors would slide down the secured messenger line, and once safely aboard the life raft, they would use a jackknife and cut the line between them and the wallowing hulk. Either plan would allow the coasties on the *Yakutat* to quickly haul in the other line, pulling the survivors and raft back to the cutter before hypothermia killed them.

Both plans also depended on the successful firing of a line from the *Yakutat* to the *Mercer*, a strategy that had ended in failure the previous night. On the one hand, Naab needed the *Yakutat* to be as close to the hulk as possible for the line not to fall short; on the other hand, the *Mercer* was swinging and pitching so wildly, he dared not get too close.

Naab brought the *Yakutat* upwind of the tanker, maneuvering as close as he dared, and shouted over the bullhorn to the survivors, "Stand by to receive a shot line—we'll secure a raft to it."

By this time, the *Mercer*'s bow was jutting out of the ocean at a 45-degree angle, with the front end completely out of the water and the broken end entirely submerged. Guldin and

Fahrner had to hang on to the outside rail tightly to keep from sliding down the sloping deck and into the foam that churned around the jagged pieces of steel where the tanker had split.

Naab positioned the *Yakutat* so that its bow was pointing directly toward the port side of the tanker. The men on board the cutter watched silently as the shooter, Wayne Higgins, prepared to fire the line. The messenger line gun was a modified Springfield rifle with a grenade charge that would fire the projectile, an 18-inch steel rod inserted in the gun's barrel. On the end of the rod, protruding from the rifle barrel, was a 13-ounce brass weight with a small circular eye attached to it, and tied to the eye was a thin messenger line. This extended back into a canister about eight inches long, mounted on the gun's barrel. The line was coiled inside the canister, ready to be taken across the seas when the projectile was fired.

"I was in the very tip of the bow," recalled Wayne later, "and I was concerned about sliding on the ice, especially because I couldn't use my hands to grip the rail, as both were needed on the rifle. I knew we had to get this line over immediately, because it looked like the broken hulk of the ship was going to sink. When I fired the gun, the recoil was tremendous, and my left hand slipped and my index finger was slashed open on the line canister. But the shot looked good."

On that first try, the line went arcing through the air, landing almost directly on top of Guldin and Fahrner. Naab motioned for the survivors to begin hauling the line in, and the raft at the other end was tossed from the cutter into the sea.

When the raft was near the *Mercer*'s bow, Fahrner and Guldin secured their end of the line, then hesitated before climbing over the rail, perhaps mustering their courage. One of the men—it's not known which—slid down the line to the water. He landed about 50 yards from the raft and clawed his way through the icy seas toward salvation. Then, when he tried to hoist himself into the raft, it capsized. Immediately, the second man, perhaps in an effort to help his shipmate, slid down the messenger line and into the ocean.

The *Yakutat* crewmen, helpless to assist the men in the water, watched as Fahrner and Guldin struggled in the breaking seas, desperately trying to get a firm grip on the raft before hypothermia made their limbs useless. For a moment, it looked like the ocean would claim two more victims, but the men fought valiantly, and both managed to grab hold of the raft, flip it right side up, and crawl aboard, collapsing on the bottom.

They were far from saved, however. The second man who jumped had not untied the line from the tanker before leaping, and now both were too frozen to open a jackknife to sever the line. This meant the raft could not be pulled to the cutter.

Communications officer Bill Bleakley, staring out a window of the *Yakutat*'s bridge at the drama unfolding, worried that the scene he had witnessed the previous night—of survivors perishing before his eyes—was going to happen again. Bleakley had not been able to forget the vision of men jumping off the tanker, and he was particularly upset when he saw one man jump and get slammed back into the hull of the tanker before crashing into the water.

Naab, who was standing next to Bleakley, said, "Now what do I do? If I back down and the line between us and the raft breaks, we've lost them." (Backing down means to reverse the engines.) "If the line between the raft and the hulk breaks, we've got them."

"You have no choice, Captain," said Bleakley. "Back down and hope."

Naab knew Bleakley was right. Any hesitation meant the men in the raft would die of hypothermia, whereas forcing a break in the line gave them a 50-50 chance of survival. The captain gave the order to back down, and every man aboard the cutter held his breath. Which line would break? Or worse, would the raft be torn apart, casting the men into the seas?

The lines tightened and rose clear of the water. A half second passed. Then a sudden cheer rang out from the men on the cutter as the line between the raft and the hulk parted! Helping hands quickly pulled the raft in, and within a couple of minutes, Guldin and Fahrner were directly below the cutter. Ropes and a scramble net were lowered. The two survivors crawled over the side of the raft and into the sea to get at the ropes, but they could barely lift their arms.

The crew of the *Yakutat*, however, had anticipated this problem, and coasties Dennis Perry and Herman Rubinsky— already wearing exposure suits—climbed down the netting and into the water. Each man went to work on a survivor, tying lines around his chest so he could be hauled up.

As Guldin and Fahrner were being hoisted, one of them became tangled in the cargo net. *Yakutat* crewman Phillip Griebel saw what was happening and, without the protection of an exposure suit, he scrambled down the cargo net to free the man. Both survivors were then safely lifted aboard the cutter.

Seconds later, a coastie pointed toward the *Mercer*'s bow and shouted, "Look! There she goes!"

The bow reared up as if it were a living thing, pointing straight toward the gray sky. Then it pivoted, falling backward into the sea in a spray of water. Only a small portion of its keel remained above the seas. Exactly 17 minutes had passed since Guldin and Fahrner leaped off the vessel.

～

To warn other ships that might be coming that way, the *Yakutat* stayed on scene with the hazardous capsized bow until it was relieved by the cutter *Unimak* that evening. Then Captain Naab ordered full steam to Portland, Maine, so the survivors could be hospitalized. All were suffering from hypothermia and frostbite, but Captain Paetzel was in the worst shape with pneumonia. Newspaper reporters were dockside as the survivors were taken off the cutter, and Fahrner calmly told the *Boston Herald*, "It was nip and tuck whether we'd make it."

The capsized bow of the *Mercer* was deemed a hazard to

navigation, and the *Unimak* later received the go-ahead to sink the half-floating hulk. Gunnery officer Ben Stabile recalled that he first fired the ship's 40-millimeter antiaircraft gun at the *Mercer*'s bow, just above the waterline "to see what would happen." Stabile was thinking that maybe the oil would leak out of the cargo holds and be replaced by water, which is heavier than oil, or that the high-explosive incendiary projectiles they shot would make the oil tanker explode and sink. When the hulk didn't move, the *Unimak*'s skipper, Captain Frank McCabe, said, "Ben, let's fire the K-guns with depth charges." Stabile had never fired live depth charges—explosives designed to detonate underwater— and the K-guns could push the explosives out only about 75 yards; all the crew wondered if this was too close for comfort.

After much discussion, it was decided that the *Unimak* should be going at full steam when Stabile fired the K-guns. That way, the cutter would be putting distance between itself and the depth charge before it exploded.

The depth charges were shaped like teardrops to better pro-pel them through the water. They measured approximately 24 inches long and 18 inches across at the wide end. The K-gun would fire the explosives in a long arc through the air, and if all went well, they would drop into the ocean close to the hulk. They were preset to explode when they reached a depth of 50 feet.

When everyone was ready, Captain McCabe wound up the engine, and the *Unimak* came flying toward the hulk at a speed of 18 knots (21 miles per hour). When the cutter was adjacent to the tanker's hull, Stabile discharged all three guns. A few seconds passed and then the charges exploded underwater, sending huge plumes of spray into the air. The *Unimak* shuddered violently, despite being a safe distance away, but the hulk of the *Mercer* barely moved.

After watching the half tanker float in the same position for 30 minutes, McCabe decided to repeat the procedure. "This time was different," said Stabile. "The hulk rose up in the air and then down she went. We breathed a big sigh of relief. We didn't want to be near that thing with night closing in. It was so hard to see. Even with radar, I worried we might hit it and become its last victims."

A MANEUVER
FOR THE AGES

One half of the *Fort Mercer* now lay at the bottom of the sea. The other half, the stern, was still afloat and being driven southward by the wind and waves. The 31 men on board felt the full range of emotions, their mood and outlook rising and falling like the half ship they were trapped on. When the tanker first broke apart, fear and confusion reigned on the stern. Arguments broke out over what to do, and the confusion showed signs of escalating into full-blown panic and chaos, especially because the men's leader, Captain Paetzel, had drifted away on the bow section of the tanker. Some talked about immediately abandoning ship in the lifeboats, while others argued the lifeboats must be a last resort. Quartermaster Luis Jomidad hedged his bets, later saying, "I went up to the boat deck and climbed into a boat with a hatchet. The release was outside the boat, and I wanted to be sure it would work, that is why I took the hatchet. One guy was crazy and screamed, 'Let's jump overboard,' but I said, 'No, wait until it sinks and then we will jump.' For the next four hours, I sat in the lifeboat with the hatchet in my hand, ready to cut the rope to release it." The quartermaster, frozen to the core, finally went back inside, but stayed up the entire night, just in case. "If it was going down," he said, "I wanted to be on the outside."

Although the *Mercer*'s stern could capsize like the bow did, the men on board were lucky that their section of the ship still had power. That meant they had operable lights, pumps, and a functioning heating system. Unfortunately, there was no radio on the stern section, and the crew had no way to communicate with the merchant ship *Short Splice*, which was standing by. The survivors had made it through Monday night, and now, on Tuesday morning, they prayed the coast guard would arrive and that their fractured ship would stay upright a little longer.

~

The storm that threatened so many lives was far from over, and on board the cutter *Eastwind*, radio operator Len Whitmore lay restless in his bunk as the ship pitched and rolled. He was on break from radio duty, but between the ship's motion and the dramatic events of the day, sleep was next to impossible, so he got out of bed, dressed, and went topside. Len learned from another crewmember that the *Mercer*'s radioman, John O'Reilly, with whom he'd been communicating prior to the tanker splitting, was dead. *Will there be more loss of life,* he asked himself, *before the* Eastwind *even arrives at the action?* He knew the cutter's crew could make a difference after all their endless training, if only they could get there in time.

With the *Eastwind* almost at the site of the *Mercer*'s stern, Len peered into the gray skies over the storm-tossed seas and wondered how Captain Petersen would go about the rescue. Len had listened in on the *Yakutat*'s radio communications as that ship attempted to rescue the men trapped on the *Mercer*'s bow, and he knew about the lives both saved and lost.

Ensign Larry White, also aboard the *Eastwind*, was equally aware of the *Yakutat*'s mixed results, and he hoped the *Eastwind*'s crew would be able to get each and every man off the *Mercer*'s stern. But he was also concerned with the manpower aboard the icebreaker, because many of the men were seasick. "We had lightened up the ship a couple weeks earlier," recalled Larry, "to get up the Hudson River to break ice. And now the *Eastwind* was really pitching and rolling. Having literally been up the river, we didn't have much time to acclimate ourselves to the sea, and a fair share of the men were too sick to perform their duties, so others had to do double work."

Larry himself was not seasick, and when the *Eastwind* was within visual range of the *Mercer*, he watched how the waves swept over the jagged end of the tanker, cascading off in waterfalls. The young ensign realized he and his shipmates would have their work cut out for them. He was surprised to see smoke coming out of the tanker's stacks, but noted how the rear of the stern sloped upward so that its propeller could be seen each time a wave swept by. As the *Eastwind* drew closer, both Larry and Len saw several of the tanker's crew standing along the deck rail, frantically waving at them. Slowly the *Eastwind* maneuvered upwind of the hulk, not wanting to be in a position where the *Mercer* could drift into the icebreaker.

Captain Petersen's first onsite decision was to establish communication with the *Mercer*. To that end, he instructed that a line with a "monkey fist" (a piece of lead or steel to add weight to the end of the line) be shot to the tanker. At the end of the line was a portable radio in a watertight container, which the seamen on the tanker were able to haul aboard. Once they removed the radio from the container, they could begin talking to the cutter. Chief engineer Jesse Bushnell, of Pasadena, Texas, the highest-ranking sailor on the tanker's stern section, told Captain Petersen that some of the men had decided to take their chances remaining on the hulk while others wanted to get off immediately. Petersen responded that he would have a rubber raft sent over. His crew fired another messenger line over to the tanker. Attached to it was a heavier line with the life raft tied in a fixed position. The other end of the line stayed with the coasties on the *Eastwind*.

When the survivors pulled their end of the line to the point where the life raft was alongside the vessel, three men immediately jumped into the sea and scrambled aboard the raft. It was not a smooth trip to the icebreaker. The seas were still on a rampage, and the *Eastwind* rolled so much that the line rode way out of the water, lifting the men and the raft high in the air. Then the raft would crash back down into the water, loosening the survivors' handholds; maintaining a good grip was the only thing that kept them from certain death in the frigid sea.

A cargo net was lowered from the *Eastwind*, and three coast guardsmen, John Courtney, Roland Hoffert, and Eugene Korpusik, volunteered to man the net, waiting by the waterline to assist the survivors. Each time the *Eastwind* rolled, the volunteers were totally dunked, but they held firm. When the raft was alongside the icebreaker, the coasties were able to tie lines around the survivors and pull them on board.

During the rescue, a second coast guard cutter, the *Acushnet*, arrived on the scene, having steamed for 24 hours into the teeth of the storm from Portland. Coastal Maine had been hit especially hard, with the Portland *Herald Press* reporting in bold headlines STORM PARALYZES STATE: STORM EQUALS WORST IN WEATHER BUREAU HISTORY. The *Acushnet* had been docked in Portland for repairs, and half its crew was scattered and marooned ashore, including its captain, John Joseph. He had been at his home in South Portland when he got the phone call about the *Pendleton* and *Mercer*: "Commander, this is the *Acushnet* calling. A message from headquarters in Boston came in. Two tankers have split up off Cape Cod, and we're to go to the rescue."

Joseph knew he'd have trouble locating his crew and responded, "Try to get the crew by telephone. If you can't get them by phone, call the local radio stations and have them broadcast a message. I'll be right there."

Easier said than done. Joseph's car stalled in the snowdrifts at Portland's Vaughn Street Bridge. It would have taken hours to walk to the pier where the *Acushnet* was docked, so he called the South Portland CG Station, and they dispatched a picket boat, which came up the river, met Joseph at the bridge, and took him to the cutter. Other crewmembers struggled through the snow, but the entire crew eventually made it, and the 210-foot *Acushnet* nosed out of Portland Harbor and headed south into the storm.

On board were two young coasties, John Mihlbauer and Sid Morris, both of whom later recalled a very rough ride to the *Mercer* and were thankful to have Captain Joseph in command. "I sure was glad to see Captain Joseph come aboard," said Morris. "He had commanded the ship admirably in several fishing boat rescues off the Grand Banks, and there was a unanimous feeling of trust and confidence by the crew for our captain, a coast guard veteran of 25 years. I knew it was going to be a bad trip, because it was difficult to maintain an upright position while we were still in the harbor. And as we sped out into open water and came abreast of the Portland Lightship, anyone who thought they might get seasick this trip was—and the others were beginning to think seriously about it." Normally the trip from Portland to the *Mercer*'s position near Nantucket took 18 hours, but because of the enormous seas, it took an additional six hours, giving everyone on board plenty of time to be seasick.

Morris remembered how he gaped in awe when he saw the

Mercer's stern. "I could see gigantic, jagged slivers of broken steel at her midsection, and a group of frantic, pleading sailors clutching the rails." John Mihlbauer remembered arriving just in time to watch the *Eastwind* haul the life raft with survivors back toward the cutter. "We could see the trouble the *Eastwind* was having with the raft," recalled Mihlbauer. "The raft was flying up, then down, and spinning too. My heart was in my mouth, knowing there were men in that raft."

Captain Joseph also watched, thinking how lucky the men in the raft were to have made it to the *Eastwind* alive. It was about this time that he started to think of another way to perform the rescue. "The way the sea was raging," said Joseph, "it looked like the stern section would soon join its forward half in Davy Jones's locker. Something had to be done fast. I went to the radio room and signaled the commander of the *Eastwind*, saying, 'Commander, I'd like to take the *Acushnet* in alongside the tanker so the survivors can jump to our deck. It's risky, but I think we can do it.'"

On the *Eastwind*, Captain Petersen, who was the on-scene commander for the entire rescue operation, hesitated before answering, weighing the risk to both the survivors and the *Acushnet* itself. The *Acushnet*, a coast guard oceangoing tug, was smaller and more maneuverable than the *Eastwind*, but still, the tactic was highly unusual, particularly in a storm. If the vessels collided due to the wildly heaving seas, the crew on the *Acushnet* could find themselves in almost as much peril as the survivors on the tanker. Captain Petersen was aware of these dangers, as well as the scrutiny he'd be under if the maneuver failed, but they were out of options. He radioed back to Captain Joseph to give it a try.

Joseph outlined his plan to his helmsman, Harvey Madigan, instructing him to turn the *Acushnet* in a semicircle, approach the tanker from the rear, and glide alongside it until ten feet remained between the two ships. Then, when the *Acushnet* was abreast of the tanker, they would stop the engines and let the cutter glide a bit closer so the survivors could jump on the fantail. Joseph added these words of caution: "Harvey, we can make it, but you've got to be careful. Don't let the bow swing into the tanker. If you do, we'll be smashed against her, surer than hell. Keep her pointed out, and we'll be okay." Both men took another moment and silently studied the current and the wind, trying to determine how fast they would drift when the propellers stopped turning.

Joseph positioned himself in the wing of the bridge, where he could see his cutter's fantail. He had Madigan slowly make the semicircle and bring the cutter toward the rear of the tanker, where he had the engines killed so he could again gauge the rate of drift. As the diesel engines fell silent, the momentum of the *Acushnet* propelled it toward the wallowing tanker looming just ahead. A thousand thoughts raced through Joseph's mind: *What if a sudden swell should smash the ships together and sink them? What if the survivors should fall between the ships and be crushed? What if the oil in the tanker should blow up upon impact? And what of my future if we fail?* The possible outcomes made him pause, but only for a second or two. "Ahead one third!" he shouted.

They were now close enough to clearly see the desperation etched into the faces of the survivors lined up at the rail of the tanker. Just then, a mountainous sea pushed the bow of the *Acushnet* toward the tanker's propeller. Madigan swung the wheel furiously, and Joseph shouted into the power-phone connected to the engine room, "Ahead on starboard, back on port," and the engines churned the ocean to even more of a froth. Just a few feet from impact, the cutter's bow stopped, and slowly began to reverse itself.

Joseph and Madigan breathed a sigh of relief, and when the *Acushnet* was directly alongside and perpendicular to the tanker, Joseph shouted, "Back on both engines!" Careful to keep the bow pointed away from the tanker, Madigan worked the wheel so that the stern of the cutter eased closer to the tanker. The distance between the *Acushnet*'s fantail and the *Mercer* closed from ten feet to just a couple feet, then a slight shudder went through the cutter as her stern hit the tanker. "Stop both engines!" Joseph shouted.

Now was the time for the survivors to jump, but not one made a move. And who could blame them? They were paralyzed with indecision, watching how the two ships, just inches apart, were rising and falling chaotically.

Coast guard lieutenant George Mahoney, Sid Morris, John Mihlbauer, and a handful of other men were out on the *Acushnet*'s rear deck, slipping and sliding, waiting for the tanker crew to jump. Mahoney screamed, "Come on, you guys, jump! We'll catch you!" Still no one even lifted a leg over the rail. The tanker and cutter were like two ends of a seesaw, and it was only for the briefest of moments that the cutter's stern rose up within three or four feet of the deck before plunging back down.

Mahoney, frustrated by the survivors' lack of action, cupped his hands around his mouth and bellowed, "Look, we can't stay here all day! Jump!"

Finally one survivor awoke from his trance, climbed over the rail, and paused, waiting for the cutter to rise on the next wave. When the cutter was three feet below him and just two feet out from the tanker, he threw himself forward and landed on the deck.

His successful leap gave the others confidence, and a second man climbed over the rail, preparing to jump. The ships were now several feet apart, and Mihlbauer put his hand forward, screaming, "No, not yet! Wait a second. Okay, now get ready. Jump!" The survivor did as he was told and made it with inches to spare, just missing being crushed to death between the ships.

Captain Joseph described what happened when the third man leaped. "He poised at the rail and then jumped. But he had waited too long. He leaped as we were falling. His feet hit our rail, and he fell backward, toward the narrowing space between the hulls of the ships. I watched, horrified, as a scream started from his lips." Two coasties lunged toward the man and grabbed him by the coat, but their momentum and the weight of the survivor began to pull them over the rail. Then three more coasties grabbed at the sliding men, and all were pulled onto the deck.

The remaining survivors were now more reluctant than ever to make the leap. Two coast guardsmen, however, acted on their own, and when the cutter rose on a swell almost level with the tanker, they simply reached out and each yanked a survivor off the *Mercer* and onto the cutter's deck. The coasties were preparing to make another grab when an especially large wave lifted the back end of the *Mercer* so high it looked like it would drop straight down on the cutter. Men scattered off the deck, fearing they'd be squashed, as Joseph screamed into the power-phone, "Full speed ahead!"

Sid Morris remembered what happened next: "The engines groaned and strained, the bulkheads and decks shivered with the sudden tearing vibration, the double screws churned furiously, and, after what seemed an eternity, our ship strained and lurched forward, away from the plunging, knifelike edges of the tanker's propeller."

The propeller came so close it actually nicked the rail. Captain Joseph, allowing himself to breathe again, decided luck was with them and ordered the helmsman to go for another try. When they were back in position, again they had to coax the survivors. Sid Morris remembers how one heavyset sailor made the leap, skidded wildly—in a standing position—across the deck, and slammed into the rail, saved only by a fast-acting coastie who grabbed him before he plunged off the ship. The survivor later told Sid the reason he slid so fast was that he had put on new shoes he wanted to save.

A total of 18 men made the leap from the tanker to the cutter, without a single casualty. Thirteen crewmembers, however, decided it was safer to stay with the tanker. Joseph had a quick message sent to headquarters:

SURVIVORS TAKEN ON BOARD BY
MANEUVERING *ACUSHNET* STERN
ALONGSIDE TANKER. MADE TWO PASSES.
RECEIVED FIVE MEN ON FIRST PASS
AND THIRTEEN ON SECOND.

Captain Joseph asked for and received permission to take the survivors to Boston, as two of them needed hospitalization. The ones who escaped without a scratch were ecstatic to be safely aboard a coast guard vessel where they could enjoy hot coffee, food, and dry clothing. "The happiest moment of my life," said quartermaster Hurley Newman, "was when I jumped onto the aft deck of the *Acushnet*."

The *Acushnet* left the accident scene at nightfall and steamed toward Boston. When Captain Joseph, his crew, and the survivors arrived in Boston at eight A.M. on Wednesday, they were all taken aback by the huge crowd gathered by the docks. A loud cheer went up from the bystanders, and car horns blared. The press was out in force, snapping pictures of survivors coming down the gangplank and shouting questions. When Captain

Joseph emerged, another cheer went up, and two survivors, Massie Hunt and Alanson Winn, got on either side of the captain, draped their arms around his shoulders, and smiled broadly as the Associated Press snapped a picture that appeared on the front page of several newspapers around the country.

Later, when Captain Joseph and the *Acushnet* arrived in Portland, another swarm of people awaited, including the captain's family. Joseph later wrote, "I came out on the wing of the bridge to receive the congratulations. As I looked down on the assembled throng and waved to my wife, my youngest son, in a loud voice, yelled, 'What's the matter, Dad? Why didn't you take them all off? Did you get chicken?'" Joseph could only smile ruefully and shake his head.

The fractured half of the *Fort Mercer* was eventually towed to New York City with the 13 crewmembers still on board. One man had to be treated for broken ribs. The ship was repaired and fitted for a new bow section and renamed the *San Jacinto*. It would remain in operation for a dozen more years before splitting in half once again and sinking during a storm off Virginia. Fortunately no lives were lost in that wreck.

TUESDAY AT CHATHAM STATION

Bernie Webber rubbed the sleep out of his tired eyes and felt a dull pain in every joint of his body. Despite his exhaustion, he had not slept well. Bernie lifted his beaten body off his bunk and looked around the room. The aches and pains reminded him what had happened. He and his brave crew had indeed saved the lives of 32 seamen in a tiny lifeboat. Bernie looked to the floor and thought he was dreaming. Dollar bills were scattered about the floor, and his dresser drawer was overflowing with cash. Not knowing what this meant, he quickly got dressed, scooped up all the money, and went downstairs. The survivors appeared to be everywhere, lying on cots and on the floor. Bernie took the money to commander Cluff.

"Where did all this cash come from?" he asked. Cluff told

him that the money was a gift collected by the *Pendleton* survivors who had managed to retrieve some of their belongings before abandoning ship. The monetary gift eventually went to buy a television set for the Chatham Station, a rare luxury in 1952.

But some others felt differently about Bernie. Higher-ups were angry about Webber's breach of protocol during the rescue—he had turned off his radio and ignored authority on the return trip to Old Harbor. Cluff told Webber that some ranking officers were even grumbling about a court-martial. But Bernie's superiors had all been shouting over one another as they attempted to give him advice. The noise had been a distraction. Bernie knew what he was doing and where he was going on that night. Cluff promised Webber that he'd handle the fallout and told him not to worry. As it happened, Cluff did not need to run interference for Bernie or anyone else. Later that day, Rear Admiral H. G. Bradbury, commander of the U.S. Coast Guard First District, sent out this priority wire:

HEARTY WELL DONE TO ALL CONCERNED WITH RESCUE OPERATIONS SS *PENDLETON.* TO BERNARD C. WEBBER BM1 IN CHARGE OF *CG 36500* AND CREW MEMBERS ANDREW J. FITZGERALD EN2, RICHARD P. LIVESEY SN, AND ERVIN E. MASKE SN. QUOTE: "YOUR OUTSTANDING SEAMANSHIP AND UTTER DISREGARD FOR YOUR SAFETY IN

CROSSING THE HAZARDOUS WATERS OF
CHATHAM BAR IN MOUNTAINOUS SEAS,
EXTREME DARKNESS AND FALLING SNOW
DURING VIOLENT WINTER GALE TO
RESCUE FROM IMMINENT DEATH THIRTY
TWO OF THE THIRTY THREE CREW
MEMBERS ON THE STRANDED STERN
SECTION OF THE ILL FATED TANKER
MINUTES BEFORE IT CAPSIZED . . .
REFLECT GREAT CREDIT ON YOU AND
THROUGH YOU THE ENTIRE SERVICE."

Richard Livesey woke up that morning with a sore throat and throbbing head. He feared that he was coming down with pneumonia. He had a week of liberty coming to him and wanted to get home as quickly as possible. But Livesey and the rest of the crew were told to stay put and wait to be examined by a doctor. Richard was relieved when the doctor informed him that he was not seriously ill. That relief quickly turned to frustration when the physician said that he still wanted to monitor Livesey and the other crewmembers for a week, which meant that his time off would be delayed.

The *Pendleton* survivors did not remain at the Chatham Lifeboat Station for very long, but they did get the opportunity to express their feelings to Webber and the crew. "I'll never forget you fellows," survivor Frank Fauteux said, shaking their hands. "God bless you, I mean it." Wiper Fred Brown nodded in agreement. Later that morning, they piled onto a bus bound for the Essex Hotel in Boston. Along the way, they had to pick up two crewmembers, 51-year-old Aaron Posvell of Jacksonville, Florida, and Tiny Myers's close friend Rollo Kennison, both of whom had been treated for shock and immersion at Cape Cod Hospital in Hyannis. The storm had blown farther out to sea before dawn. As the bus left the Chatham Station, the seamen drove past the wreckage of their ship glistening in the morning sun. "There she is," young Carroll Kilgore said, with sadness in his voice.

One of Boston's major newspapers, the *Daily Record*, ran the bold headline 32 RESCUED, 50 CLING TO SPLIT SHIPS OFF CAPE. The Cape Cod *Standard-Times* ran the headline announcing FOUR CHATHAM COAST GUARDS RESCUE 32 AS TWO TANKERS BREAK OFF CAPE. The front page of the *Boston Daily Globe* reported 32 SAVED OFF TANKERS. The newspaper also ran a photo of skipper John J. Fitzgerald with the subhead "Boston Captain Dies on Pendleton Bow." This declaration was a bit premature, since the Fitzgerald family was still under the impression he might be alive.

Margaret Fitzgerald had first received word that her husband was in trouble on the evening of February 18. The tanker captain's 11-year-old son, John J. Fitzgerald III, heard the telephone ring while he and his brother were watching *The Adventures of Kit Carson* on television. His mother took the call and then listened silently as the disturbing news was relayed.

"My God," Margaret screamed. "Did my husband die?"

The person on the other end of the call told her that it was still a fluid and confusing situation. He told her about the four simultaneous rescue operations and that at this point, her husband's fate was not known. Margaret Fitzgerald hung up the telephone, tried to regain her composure, and gathered her four children to break the news. Like his siblings, young John had a difficult time understanding what his mother was trying to say. It was inconceivable that his father would not come home. Although the boy had grown accustomed to prolonged absences— the tanker captain was home only 45 days out of the year—he expected his dad to walk through their front door eventually, his arms full of presents. His mother, meanwhile, made arrangements for her children and then headed down to Chatham.

Millie Oliviera was the only wife waiting inside the Hotel Essex lobby when the tired survivors came pouring out of the bus after their two-and-a-half-hour ride to Boston. Flanked by two of her three children, she embraced her husband, Aquinol, as he stepped out of the cold and into the warm lobby. During those long hours stranded on the stern, the thin, bespectacled cook feared that he'd never see his family again. Aquinol Oliviera and his 31 crewmates were given free accommodations at the Hotel Essex while they waited to give their statements during the coast guard's impending inquiry. Before that, however, the survivors also had to describe their harrowing ordeal to eager Boston-area reporters. During an interview with the *Boston Post*, Aquinol said he was baking at the moment the ship split and that his face was covered with flour when he ran topside to see what had happened. He also said the storm was worse than anything the Germans had dropped on his ship during the invasion of Sicily nine years before. Rollo Kennison carried a triangular paper parcel when he spoke with reporters. Asked what it was, Kennison reached in and pulled out the flare gun Tiny Myers had given him before his death. "He was too good to die," a still-shaken Kennison told members of the press.

~

Margaret Fitzgerald walked the beach the next morning with her arms folded to fight off the cold. She stared out at the whipping waves, heartbroken that her husband was missing and presumed dead. She was not alone. Hundreds of people had driven down to the bluff at Chatham that day to see the *Pendleton* wreckage. The crowd was so large that special police patrols had to be called in to direct traffic. For many onlookers, the image of the shredded stern provided an ominous reminder of the power of the sea. There were others, though, who gazed at the wreckage and saw opportunity.

Rumors sprouted up that a small fortune had been left behind on one of the tables inside the stern. The story was that a group of seamen were engaged in a heated game of cards when they were notified that a lifeboat was approaching the ship. As crewmembers began to gather up their money, one player reminded the others of the sailors' superstition that says a man who picks up the stakes while abandoning ship will one day fall victim to the sea himself. The rumor might have started because the survivors later had enough cash with them to stuff Bernie Webber's sock drawer and cover the floor around his bunk. Nonetheless, the story had many true believers among the Chatham fishermen, who were also tempted by the ship's fully equipped machine shop, expensive navigational equipment, and large clothing supply. The coast guard said it would not patrol the two sections of the *Pendleton* unless ordered to do so. Such orders never came, so in keeping with the scavenger tradition of the outer Cape, David Ryder and others ventured out into the rough waters in search of treasure. Ryder used his own 38-foot-long liner, the *Alice & Nancy*, to get up close to the stern while a couple of friends climbed aboard and picked at its carcass. Ryder refused to go on board and watched as the other men slipped along the oily deck. Among the items liberated from the wreckage was the *Pendleton*'s red jib, a triangular sail located in front of the mast, which remains in the Ryder family to this day.

THE SEARCH OF THE
PENDLETON BOW

In the days following the disaster, crews from the Chatham Lifeboat Station made several attempts to board the bow section of the *Pendleton*, which was now grounded in 54 feet of water near the Pollock Rip Lightship, almost seven miles off the Chatham coast. "It looks a little choppy out there," commander Daniel Cluff told reporters two days after the rescue. "But I think we'll make a try at boarding her anyway." However, sea conditions remained rough and prevented crewmembers from climbing aboard the unsteady vessel. In the meantime, crews carried out beach patrols searching for bodies that might have washed up onshore. None were found.

The weather finally broke on Sunday, February 24, almost a full week after the ship had split in two. Richard Livesey, Mel

Gouthro, coxswain Chick Chase, and two other coasties from the Chatham Lifeboat Station joined seamen from the salvage tug *Curb* as they pulled up alongside the bow section of the *Pendleton*. The hulk had drifted to almost the exact spot where the Pollock Rip Lightship was anchored, and the lightship had been moved a couple days earlier for fear the bow would collide with it. The *Pendleton* bow floated more or less upright, with the tip rising from the water at a 45-degree angle. The seas were calm now, and the men managed to get aboard the vessel with relative ease. Richard Livesey remained on the lifeboat, however; he could still see the face of Tiny Myers in his mind's eye. The image haunted him in his sleep and nearly every waking moment.

Livesey did not know what horror awaited the lifeboat men as they searched the bow of the *Pendleton*, but he did know that it was something he could not witness again. Mel Gouthro wasn't wild about climbing on the hulk either: "We were a little afraid to go on that hunk of steel, not knowing when it might shift."

Nevertheless, he and the others climbed aboard, coming from the broken end and climbing hand over hand up the steep-angled deck. They moved gingerly along the railing because one false step would surely mean an unexpected trip into the icy water below. The temperature was still in the 20s, but the sun was bright, and that offered them much-needed light as they began their search. Then they used flashlights as they entered the bowels of the ship. "It was eerie," recalls Gouthro, "because the ship was making all kinds of rumbling noises, perhaps from where the seas were hitting the area where the boat had split."

The men scoured the broken vessel and found no bodies above the ship's waterline. It appeared that Captain John Fitzgerald and his seven-member crew had all been washed away. This thought vanished quickly when Mel Gouthro and crew approached the forecastle, where they made a sad discovery.

They entered the compartment slowly, their flashlights drawn to the figure of a man stretched out on a paint locker shelf. It was clear he was dead. He was covered in newspaper, in an apparent attempt to ward off hypothermia. Each of his feet was stuck inside sawdust bags, and his shoes and socks were found on the floor. The man had had no access to blankets, because all the crew's quarters, bunks, and galley were in the stern. It seemed the crewmember had barricaded himself in the forward locker room and had not been able to hear or see the rescue boats that had come to save him six days earlier.

"He had a frozen look on his face," Gouthro recalls. "That young man was scared to death. What a lonely way to die." Gouthro surmised that the sailor might have been the lookout before the split, stationed at the very front of the ship with a foghorn ready to sound if he saw another vessel.

A search of the dead seaman's body yielded a driver's license identifying him as 25-year-old Herman G. Gatlin of Greenville, Mississippi. Positive identification came later by comparing fingerprints of the dead man's left thumb with that found on the back of the man's identification card.

Gatlin was brought back to Chatham Station and placed in an outbuilding until the coroner arrived. The doctor concluded that the cause of death was exposure and shock and, surprisingly, that the time of death was during the first day of the shipwreck: "Died before 2400 [midnight] 2/18/52."

What happened to Captain Fitzgerald and the other men on the bow will remain a mystery. Were they swept off the ship shortly after it split in two? Did they fall off the catwalk trying to reach the forwardmost part of the ship, as radioman John O'Reilly had on the *Mercer* bow? Or were they killed at the moment of the accident, as one surviving seaman, Oliver Gendron, surmised? When the ship first cracked in half, Gendron said, "a 70-foot wave lifted us till the bow pointed straight up. Then we came down, and there was a grinding, tearing crash. As we hit the trough of the wave, the mast came down. It crashed into the midship house. I should have been there, but I was aft at a pinochle game." Gendron added that he believed the mast stunned, injured, or killed the men in the midship house, including Captain Fitzgerald.

Gendron could be right, but the only person who might have seen what happened to Captain Fitzgerald and the rest of the men was Herman Gatlin, whose lifeless body now lay in the Chatham Station.

PART III

BEING LABELED A HERO
CAN BE A BURDEN

In the months following the rescue, Bernie Webber and his crewmen found themselves riding a different wave, one of public adulation. This proved to be an equally difficult task for the young coasties, none of whom had ever sought the spotlight. Their ascension from brave men who merely did their jobs to media darlings was dictated somewhat by the news of the day. The Korean War continued to drag on as armistice talks between the United States and North Korea remained at a stalemate. In fact, on February 18, the day of the *Pendleton* rescue, 17 American soldiers were killed in action, including seven servicemen from the 224th Regiment, 40th Infantry Division. War-weary American citizens needed something to feel good about, something to rally around. The men of *CG 36500* provided them with a diversion from the harsh realities of war.

Bernie Webber reunited briefly with Andy Fitzgerald, Ervin Maske, and Richard Livesey in Washington, DC, on May 14, 1952. They had traveled to the nation's capital to receive the U.S. Coast Guard's highest honor, the Gold Lifesaving Medal. The crewmembers were happy to see one another and knew how fortunate they were to be awarded such a prestigious medal. The ceremony would never have taken place had it not been for the great persistence on Bernie Webber's part. A few days after the rescue, he had been called into commander Cluff's office and handed the telephone.

On the other line was an official from coast guard headquarters who first congratulated Bernie on the rescue and then informed him that he would be awarded the Gold Lifesaving Medal.

"What about my crew?" Webber asked.

"They will all receive the Silver Lifesaving Medal," the official replied.

Bernie's anger and exhaustion erupted over the phone line. "I think it stinks," he shouted into the receiver. "They were there, the same as me, and did all the heavy rescuing. If they can't get the gold, then I don't want it." Cluff was visibly upset hearing one of his men talk that way to an official.

"You can't be serious?" the startled official asked.

Webber said he was and drew a line in the sand. He repeated that if his men couldn't get the medal, he wouldn't accept it.

Coast guard officials gave in to Webber's ultimatum, knowing the public relations nightmare they would have on their hands if they turned their backs on the new hero. Bernie and his men cherished the medal, which can be granted to any member of the U.S. military who conducts a rescue within U.S. waters or those waters subject to U.S. jurisdiction and who carries out the rescue at "extreme peril and risk of life."

~

The wreck of the *Pendleton* sat off the coast of Chatham, Massachusetts, in two pieces for nearly 26 years, providing boaters a disturbing reminder of the worst the sea had to offer. For thousands of years, the ocean had offered its bounty and collected its debts. That toll would be paid by the men swallowed by the sea and by those they left behind.

Like the relatives of the other doomed crewmen, the family of *Pendleton* captain John J. Fitzgerald was left wondering why the ocean that had given them so much had taken even more. Yet instead of being repelled by the sight of the wreck, the captain's family was drawn to it. Countless times over the next several years, John J. Fitzgerald's widow, Margaret, bundled her four children into the family car for the 87-mile trip from Roslindale to Chatham. It was Margaret's way of keeping her husband's memory alive for the children. Their son John became so enamored with the area that he decided to call it home. He would later raise a family in Chatham, and his own son eventually answered the call to the sea, fishing in the same waters that had claimed his grandfather's life so many years before.

~

There had been attempts to salvage the remains of the *Pendleton*, which had a scrap metal value of about $60,000. During the 1950s, the remains were also a concern for environmentalists, who feared additional release of oil from the fractured tanker would ruin local beaches and destroy wildlife. John F. Kennedy, then a United States Senator, insisted that salvage operations would have to be approved and supervised by both the United States Coast Guard and the Army Corps of Engineers. As it happened, the oil leaked out slowly over the next 30 years.

The Army Corps of Engineers would later play the lead role in sinking the structures once and for all. The infamous Blizzard of 1978 shredded what was left of the *Pendleton*'s superstructure abovewater. The wreck became a menace to navigation, since the stern was now submerged and hidden from the view of those piloting small craft in the busy area off Chatham. Contractors were called in to cut away much of the steel before it was blown up by the Army Corps of Engineers and buried where it sat, just three miles off Monomoy.

THE INQUIRY

For the surviving members of the *Pendleton* crew, the feelings of relief and joy for having lived through the tragedy were now replaced by anger. They allowed their bitterness to flow during a coast guard inquiry hearing that began on February 20, 1952, at Constitution Base in Charlestown, Massachusetts. A three-man fact-finding panel listened as one survivor after another stood up and told how they had been doomed to fail during 12 torturous hours on the open sea. A major concern was that a fracture in the ship had been discovered one month prior, in January 1952, but had gone unrepaired.

The most scathing testimony came from crewmembers who told the panel that much of the ship's equipment was in poor working order. For instance, survivors testified that no distress signals could be found on the ship. Witnesses also reported that smoke signals and many of the ship's flares did not work. Even getting off the ship had proved to be an arduous task for crew-members, because the single Jacob's ladder available had only three rungs. The ship's construction was still the most glaring flaw. After hearing much of the testimony, panel member Captain William Storey surmised that extreme cold and violent motion in heavy sea, combined with locked-up stresses in the welded metal, may have caused the disasters on both ships. The testimony of men such as *Fort Mercer* crewmember John Braknis supported Storey's deduction. He told investigators he had heard strange rumblings, like the sound of welds splitting, a full four hours before the tanker broke up.

With regard to the SS *Pendleton*, the Marine Board of Investigation concluded that "the tank steamer incurred a major structural failure resulting in a complete failure of the hull girder and causing the vessel to break in two in the way of the number seven and number eight cargo tanks and resulting in the loss of nine lives."

Despite testimony to the contrary, the board also concluded "that the *Pendleton* was manned and equipped in accordance with the certificate of inspection. . . ." The panel did acknowledge, however, that of four orange smoke signals used by crewmembers on the stern section, only one was able to fire. Investigators also concluded that 12 of the ship's parachute flares fired into the air normally, but that only a single flare illuminated the snow-swept sky.

Ultimately, the board concluded that three principal factors led to the break of the SS *Pendleton*: construction, weather, and cargo loading. Regarding the ship's construction, investigators concluded, "Due to its welded construction and design, there were many points of stress concentration in the *Pendleton*." The board pointed especially to what appeared to be defective welding in brackets in the middle of the ship.

As for the weather, the Marine Board of Investigation simply amplified what the survivors of the *Pendleton* and the four men who had saved them already knew. Investigators wrote,

```
THE BOARD IS OF THE OPINION THAT
THE WEATHER PLAYED A VITAL PART IN
CAUSING THE CASUALTY, PARTICULARLY
THE TEMPERATURE AND THE SEA. THERE
WAS A NORTHEASTERLY GALE BLOWING
AT THE TIME WITH VERY ROUGH SEAS
AND THE POSSIBLE POSITION OF THE
VESSEL WITH REFERENCE TO THE
DIRECTION OF THE SEAS WOULD AT
TIMES PLACE THE BOW AND STERN OF
THE VESSEL IN THE CRESTS OF WAVES
WITH LITTLE OR NO SUPPORT
AMIDSHIP.
```

The panel also concluded that the ship changed to a southerly course after getting pounded by several heavy seas until she finally split in two. They acknowledged that the low temperature of the seawater, listed as approximately 38 degrees Fahrenheit, contributed to the brittle fractures.

The intense storm was the fault of Mother Nature alone, unlike the loading of the ship, which was the result of human error. The probe found the loading of the tanker had an "adverse effect" that caused the ship to sag, which created more tension at the bottom of the vessel. According to the report, the tanks in the forward end of the ship, excluding 120 barrels of fuel oil in the port deep tank, were empty. The number nine tank was nearly empty as well, and the aft water tanks were only partially filled. This put the majority of the weight in the midship section, where the oil tanks were full. The resulting "sagging effect" was "badly aggravated by the extremely heavy seas." Despite this finding, the board did acknowledge that the ship was loaded in line with the usual practice in the tanker trade.

In the end, the sinking of the SS *Pendleton* would be chalked up to fate, and no one would be held accountable by the Marine Board of Investigation. They concluded, "There was no incompetence, misconduct, unskillfullness or willful violation of the law or any rule or regulation on the part of any licensed officers, or seamen, employers, owner or agent of the vessel or any inspector or officer of the Coast Guard which contributed to this casualty." To many of the survivors, the report appeared to be a governmental whitewash.

The panel did recommend a study be conducted on the best way to load T2 tankers to minimize sagging. Investigators also recommended that a vertical ladder be installed on the forward side of the bridge structure to allow the captain and crew an emergency exit from the bridge to the deck or the catwalk forward.

Finally, the board noted it was in hearty accordance with the commendations that were being awarded to "various officers and men of the Coast Guard who participated in the successful rescue of members of the *Pendleton* crew."

A similar inquiry into the *Fort Mercer* split came to the same conclusions.

THE RESTORATION

November 1981

S he sat unnoticed, this once proud vessel, now a mere shell of her former self. Those who walked by paid little mind. If anything, she was a nuisance, and no doubt there were some who thought she should have been scrapped years ago. Her canvas was rotted, and her paint had chipped away. Squirrels and other small creatures had built their nests in her manifold, and the tops of her cabins were badly worn by years of neglect. The *CG 36500* had been put up on blocks and left unprotected from the elements for 13 years behind a maintenance garage on the property of the Cape Cod National Seashore. Surrounded by sand, shrubs, and small pine trees, the historic boat that had saved so many lives was in need of being rescued herself.

The "old thirty-six" model lifeboat had been decommissioned in 1968 and replaced by the newer 44-foot twin 180-horsepower diesel all-steel lifeboat. Although the 36ers were still considered reliable, the 44-footers were faster and could carry nearly double the number of passengers. Most 36-footers were destroyed, but the Chatham lifeboat had been given a reprieve. Because she was a Gold Medal lifesaving vessel, the *CG 36500* was handed over to the Cape Cod National Seashore, and initially, there were bold plans to preserve the lifeboat. Officials there wanted to make the vessel part of a small museum, but a lack of funding and foresight doomed the project. The boat was now nothing more than an eyesore taking up space on government property. The *CG 36500* had been victimized by the blazing sun of more than a dozen summers and the snow and sleet of those raw Cape Cod winters. Her caregivers had even neglected to provide any kind of protective tarp cover. It was a sad sight. Something that had meant so much to so many had outlasted its usefulness and its own legend. The story may have faded away into the heavy fabric of outer Cape folklore if it had not been for the determination of a group of local men who fought to restore the boat to its former glory.

Their leader was Bill Quinn, a freelance television cameraman and longtime friend of Dick Kelsey, the photographer whose pictures of the *Pendleton* rescue remain etched in the collective memories of those fortunate enough to remember the Gold Medal Crew. Quinn first saw the boat while he and his son were attending an auction of used vehicles sponsored by the Cape Cod National Seashore. He was looking for a sturdy automobile with room to store his camera equipment and a big engine that would allow him to respond rapidly to any breaking news story. As he was inspecting the jeeps, trucks, and other vehicles, the tired old boat caught his eye. Being a former navy man with a fondness for boats and ships, Quinn was immediately intrigued. He walked over for a closer look and noticed the faded numbers painted near her bow. Quinn could barely contain his excitement and waved his son over. "Look at that!" he said, pointing. "That's the boat that saved all those men." The need for a new vehicle seemed like an afterthought now. Quinn knew he had been brought here for a reason. Shocked by the lack of care and attention paid to the historic vessel, he dreamed up a plan on the spot; he just had to save the lifeboat. The question was, could she be saved?

~

Quinn left the Cape Cod National Seashore and returned later with a friend who specialized in boat repair. The friend had brought an ice pick and began jabbing the vessel from stem to stern. Quinn's dream of restoring the lifeboat would be dashed if the vessel had rotted out. But despite its ragged outward appearance, the men were surprised to find very little rot in the wooden boat. The only small areas of concern were in the engine room and the stern's tow post. Underneath her rough facade, the *CG 36500* was still a healthy lifeboat. For once, Quinn was thankful the boat had been in the possession of the Cape Cod National Seashore for all those years. Although it had been left outside, the vessel sat on government property and therefore had never been vandalized. Yes, this once proud lifeboat could rise from the ashes, but Bill Quinn knew he couldn't do it alone.

Quinn first approached the Chatham Historical Society to see if it would be willing to take guardianship of the dilapidated lifeboat. Despite its clear historical significance, society members feared that restoring and maintaining such a boat would be like free-falling into a bottomless money pit. "Who'll pay for the restoration and the continuous upkeep?" they asked. Chatham's loss turned into Orleans's gain as the neighboring town's historical society agreed to accept the vessel if the Cape Cod National Seashore was willing to give it up. Quinn met with government officials, who at first agreed to turn the boat over, but only on permanent loan. Quinn kept after them, though, until a deal was worked out giving him legal ownership of the lifeboat. He deeded the vessel over to the Orleans Historical Society and began enlisting local craftsmen for the important job of rebuilding the boat.

Quinn had no shortage of volunteers and needed very little effort to galvanize them for this mission. To the people of Chatham, Orleans, and Harwich, the small lifeboat was not only a legend, it was a testament to the spirit of Cape Cod. Ruggedness and reliability were shared traits of both the boat and the hardy people who carved out their lives along the sandy, windswept shores at the easternmost tip of the United States.

A small group of men gathered at the National Seashore on a chilly November morning in 1981 to witness the rebirth of this vessel. They watched intently as a large crane hoisted the lifeboat from its cradle, awakening her from a 13-year slumber. The small craft was placed on a flatbed truck and taken to a garage in Orleans, where the volunteers went to work. They realized quickly the amount of sweat and skill it would take to pull the project off. The goal was to finish it in five to six months, and that would mean thousands of hours of labor. It was a community coming together for a common cause. These volunteers spanned generations; they were both young and old, and yet all had been touched in some way by the *CG 36500*. One volunteer remembered being towed by the vessel as a kid when his boat ran into trouble on the Bass River. It was now time to repay that debt and preserve this floating piece of history for generations to come.

The first order of business was to see if the boat's GM-471 engine could be saved. Surprisingly, it was still usable, although in need of some serious work. The engine was taken out and shipped up to Boston, where it was rebuilt by marine mechanics free of charge. The engine block's crane shaft was reconditioned, and the cylinders, connecting rods, and bearings were replaced. Every screw in the lifeboat's hull had to be taken out and replaced with a larger one. Workers used scrapers to chip away what was left of the paint, and then sanded the vessel down to the bare wood before refurbishing both the side and bottom planks. All of this hard work nearly went up in smoke when the Orleans Fire Department was called to the garage one evening. An oil burner had malfunctioned, and many feared the lifeboat would burn like kindling. Fortunately, she suffered no real damage, apart from being covered with oil that was easily cleaned off.

While the volunteers were busy with the boat, Bill Quinn was saddled with the equally difficult task of finding money to pay for materials, upkeep, and the like. He contacted a reporter at the *Cape Cod Times*, who wrote an article about the restoration project, and soon the much-needed funds started flowing in. The Chatham Historical Society even chipped in some cash to keep the project afloat. Quinn and his group raised more than $10,000, and an equal amount in materials, to realize their dream.

After six months, the volunteers had met their goal. The lifeboat was fully restored and repainted, with her famous letters reappearing boldly near the bow. It was now time to see if the "old thirty-six" was seaworthy. An official relaunching ceremony was held at Rock Harbor in Orleans, where the lifeboat resides today. The relaunching of this famous boat would not be complete without the presence of its equally famous coxswain. Bernie Webber took time off from his job as a tugboat captain and, with his wife, Miriam, drove up to Cape Cod from their home in Florida to be reunited with the small craft that had saved the lives of so many on that torturous winter night years before.

The *CG 36500* remains a living museum dedicated to the lifesavers of Cape Cod. She is in the water year-round, with her winter storage at the Stage Harbor Marina in Chatham. During the summer, the lifeboat occupies a berth at Rock Harbor and travels to various boat shows around the region, where her legend is retold to a new generation of New Englanders. At her helm is Pete Kennedy, a member of the Orleans Historical Society and a man dedicated to keeping the spirit of this tiny boat and the Gold Medal Crew alive. When he's out on the lifeboat by himself in eight- to ten-foot seas, Kennedy can't help but think of Webber, Andy Fitzgerald, Richard Livesey, and Ervin Maske. "They saw waves seven times as large," he marvels. "It's incomprehensible to me that they could perform that well under those conditions. What a remarkable feat for those young men."

Epilogue
THEY WERE YOUNG ONCE

In the years following the *Pendleton* rescue, Bernie Webber and Richard Livesey saw each other on occasion at Cape Cod, and the conversation usually focused on their families. One topic they *never* discussed was the tumultuous hours they had spent huddled together on that small wooden craft cheating death on Chatham Bar. When the idea first came for a 50th reunion of the Gold Medal Crew, Bernie Webber was against it. He didn't want to relive the past. He would be the focus of attention and adulation, and he felt a little guilty and possibly a little scared. While friends and strangers would be praising him for his heroic effort, Webber feared the dark memories of the death of George "Tiny" Myers. Could he prepare himself for that?

Another concern was whether such an event would be good for the coast guard. Webber may have felt used by the coast guard during his countless public relations appearances in the months following the rescue, but he also realized the service had been fair to him overall, and he didn't want to take part in anything that would make a mockery of his life's work. Organizers convinced Webber that such a reunion would be done tastefully.

Bernie also wanted to make sure that the three members of his crew would attend. There could be no reunion of the Gold Medal Crew if all four men were not present. Webber had been fighting for recognition for his crew since the day he had nearly declined the Gold Lifesaving Medal back in 1952. That ceremony still stuck in his craw so many years later. Miriam had not been invited to attend, nor had any relatives of the other crewmembers. Webber told organizers that family members would have to be invited this time around. Those planning the reunion agreed to Webber's request and promised him that their travel expenses would be taken care of.

Ervin Maske had misgivings of his own. He had undergone knee replacement surgery about a year before, and standing for long periods of time put tremendous stress on his body. He knew there would be a lot of standing around at a reunion like this. Like Bernie, he also knew that he might be forced to relive the rescue over again in his mind. Ervin had spent decades keeping those memories at arm's length.

For their parts, Andy Fitzgerald and Richard Livesey were both excited to take part in such a reunion. The festivities began on May 12, 2002, and were spread out over several days with events in Boston and on Cape Cod. Captain W. Russell

Webster, chief of operations for the First District U.S. Coast Guard in Boston, spearheaded the planning and managed to track down all the crewmembers and even one survivor from the SS *Pendleton*. Charles Bridges had been just 18 years old when his life was saved on that frigid night so many years before. Bridges now had a wife, a daughter, and a 20-acre farm in his native North Palm Beach, Florida.

They had been young once, all willing to risk their lives for their job, for others in need. Now here they were in the twilight of their years. All had tried to put the rescue behind them, seeing it as a chapter in the book of their lives, but not the defining moment. After all, there had been weddings, the births of children, and, sadly, the death of a child as well. Yet as they spoke, it became clear that the bond between these men was as strong as ever.

For Bernie Webber, the most emotional moment of the reunion came when he saw Ervin. The man could barely stand and yet did his best to smile through the pain. Maske had always held a special place in Bernie's heart. He was the one member of the patchwork crew who did not have to be on that suicide mission. Ervin had held no real allegiances to Webber and his men; he was merely at the Chatham Lifeboat Station awaiting a ride back to his lightship. Ordinary men might have kept quiet, minded their own business, and stayed out of the fray, but Ervin Maske proved to be no ordinary man. Now, a half century later, it was time for Bernie to say thank you. He approached Maske with his voice cracking and wrapped him in a tearful embrace. Maske's daughter, Anita Jevne, felt her own eyes watering as she saw the love that was shown to her father. The reunion was an eye-opening experience for Anita, who had never been told the details of that traumatic night. "My dad always said it was no big deal," Jevne recalled. "He said it was just his job and that he did what he had to do. Once I heard the story told at the reunion, I was a bit in awe of my father and of the other three men."

The celebration culminated with a brief voyage on the CG *36500*. The crewmembers all smiled as they climbed aboard, although one of them expressed reservations. "Why do we have to go on that boat?" Ervin asked his daughter. He had done his best to stay out of the water since finishing his coast guard enlistment, and now here he was stepping onto a boat that may have saved lives, but that had also left him with decades of nightmares, according to his wife. Maske did not share his feelings with anyone else as he took a seat on the boat and braced himself for what was to come.

Despite the fact that it was the middle of spring, the air was cold, the winds were strong, and the water was a bit choppy. Still, the crew could have only wished for weather like this during the last trip they had made together on this boat. They left the Chatham Fish Pier for a brief journey around the harbor. *Pendleton* survivor Charles Bridges watched the small parade of boats circling around the harbor from the pier. Two coast guard officers from the current generation also rode on the CG *36500* to provide a helpful hand if something went wrong. But nothing went wrong on this day. Bernie Webber once again took his rightful place behind the wheel. The *CG 36500* was flanked by two 44-foot motor lifeboats and a 27-foot surf rescue boat. The young coast guardsmen on those vessels, no doubt knowing they might someday be tested to the limits of their endurance, looked on with great pride.

~

At the time, the *Pendleton* and *Fort Mercer* rescues were the largest rescues performed by the coast guard. They would later be surpassed by the rescues involved with the cruise vessel *Prinsendam* in the Gulf of Alaska in 1980 and New Orleans's Hurricane Katrina in 2005. The *Pendleton* and *Fort Mercer* are still the largest open-sea rescues involving small boats and cutters in U.S. maritime history.

SOME FINAL NOTES ABOUT THE RESCUERS

Andy Fitzgerald
Andy Fitzgerald is the last surviving member of the Gold Medal Crew. He and his wife, Gloria, live in Colorado. Andy was asked to be the guest speaker at the United States Coast Guard's Annual Prayer Breakfast at the U.S. Coast Guard Command Center in Washington, DC, in 2009. "I was always told not to

begin a story with the words 'it was a dark and stormy night,'"
he told several hundred guests in attendance. "But it really was!"
he added, triggering a chorus of applause and laughter.

RICHARD LIVESEY

Richard Livesey passed away on December 28, 2007. He worked
several jobs after his years in the coast guard, including as a jani-
tor at a high school. No one besides his closest family members
knew of his role in the heroic rescue of 1952. He recalled his
days spent at Chatham Station as especially happy times, not
because of the rescue but because of the friendships.

ERVIN MASKE

Ervin Maske died on October 7, 2003. By this time, he was
working part-time as a school bus driver in his hometown of
Marinette, Wisconsin. Maske was going to pick up the kids that
morning and made it across the railroad tracks just beyond the
bus yard when his heart gave out and he collapsed at the steering
wheel. "My dad always wore his coast guard cap while driving
the bus," Anita Jevne said. "He wasn't wearing it on that day.
Maybe he knew he wouldn't be coming home."

BERNIE WEBBER

Bernie Webber died in 2009 at his home in Melbourne, Florida,
just two days after he had sent an e-mail to the authors of this
book, along with a photo of the refurbished *CG 36500* that
read, "Guys—here's your boat—if a movie is made, she'll be

ready. Just like brand new. I won't be around, but give her a kiss for me." Webber was 80 years old. In 2011, the U.S. Coast Guard honored Webber with a ship in his name. The *Bernard C. Webber* was launched in April 2011. She commenced her sea trials on November 27, 2011. She arrived in her homeport of Miami, Florida, on February 6, 2012, and was commissioned on April 14, 2012, at the Port of Miami. The ship's motto reflects the character of the man: "Determination heeds no interference."

SELECTED BIBLIOGRAPHY

GOVERNMENT AGENCY REPORTS

United States Coast Guard. "Marine Board of Investigation into disappearance of fishing vessel PAOLINA, with all persons onboard, off Atlantic Coast, February 1952," February 16, 1952.

———. "Marine Board of Investigation; structural failure of tanker FORT MERCER off Cape Cod on February 18, 1952, with loss of life," February 25, 1952.

———. "Marine Board of Investigation; structural failure of tanker PENDLETON off Cape Cod on February 18, 1952, with loss of life," February 25, 1952.

———. Operational Immediate Dispatch from CGC MCCULOCH to CCGD ONE, February 18, 1952.

———. Operational Immediate Dispatch from CHATHAM MASS LBS to ZEN/CCGDONE, February 19, 1952.

———. Priority Dispatch from COMEASTAREA to USCGC *Eastwind*, February 18, 1952.

———. Priority Dispatch from CCDG ONE to COGUARD CHATHAM LBS, February 19, 1952.

———. Priority Dispatch from NODA/CGC MCCULOCH to HIPS/CCGD ONE, February 19, 1952.

Newspaper and Wire Service Articles

"6 More Die Leaping for Life Rafts." *Boston American*, February 19, 1952.

"Smashed Lifeboat Found [*Paolina*]." *Boston Globe*, February 17, 1952.

"Five Deaths in Wild Northeaster." *Boston Globe*, February 18, 1952.

"Storm Ties Up N.E." *Boston Globe*, February 18, 1952.

"Maine Rescuers Fight Toward 1,000 Stranded" and "Crewmen Abandon Storm-Struck Craft." *Boston Globe*, Special Edition, February 18, 1952.

"32 Saved Off Tankers," "33 Deaths, Huge Loss Caused by N.E. Storm," "20,000 Marooned," "6 Crewmen on Fort Mercer Believed Lost," "Hero Rescuers Took Terrific Beating," and "46 in Peril." *Boston Globe*, February 19, 1952.

"Rescued Seamen Tell Stories" and "Pendleton Cut Speed Before She Split in Two." *Boston Globe*, February 20, 1952.

"An Epic Job." *Boston Globe*, February 23, 1952.

"Unusual Leaks on Fort Mercer, Mate Testifies." *Boston Globe*, February 26, 1952.

"First a Roar, Then She Split." *Boston Herald*, February 19, 1952.

"32 Saved, 50 Missing, Two Perish as 2 Tankers Break Up Off Cape." *Boston Herald*, February 19, 1952.

"Cloth Rope Saved Four." *Boston Herald*, February 20, 1952.

"Pendleton's Survivors Tell of Harrowing Ordeal at Sea." *Boston Herald*, February 20, 1952.

"70 Saved, 14 Dead After 2 Ships Split." *Boston Herald*, February 20, 1952.

"Half Tanker Bucks Gale." *Boston Herald*, February 22, 1952.

"Tugs Pulling Stern" and "Mercer Crew Score Leadership." *Boston Globe*, February 22, 1952.

"Fort Mercer Stern Arrives Safely in Newport." *Boston Herald*, February 23, 1952.

"1500 Marooned" and "Split Bow, Stern of 1 Craft Sighted." *Boston Herald*, February 18, 1952.

"Maine Snow-bunk Entombs Sleepy Tar in Car 54 Hours" and "Storm Death Toll Set at 31." *Boston Herald*, February 21, 1952.

"Broken Tanker First Noticed on Radar." *Boston Herald*, February 26, 1952.

"13 Refuse to Quit Hulk of Tanker—58 Saved." *Boston Post*, February 20, 1952.

"40 on Tanker Sections." *Boston Traveler*, February 19, 1952.

"18 Tanker Men Here." *Boston Traveler*, February 20, 1952.

"Salvage Tugs Move in to Tow Broken Hulks" and "Admiral Lauds 4 in Epic Small Boat Rescue." *Boston Traveler*, February 20, 1952.

"Four Chatham Coast Guards Rescue 32." *Cape Cod Standard-Times*, February 19, 1952.

"Coast Guards Save 18 Men Off Nantucket." *Cape Cod Standard-Times*, February 20, 1952.

"Storm Tossed Dragger Safe." *Cape Cod Standard-Times*, February 20, 1952.

"Fact Finding Panel Takes Testimony." *Cape Cod Standard-Times*, February 21, 1952.

"Tanker Stern Being Towed." *Cape Cod Standard-Times*, February 23, 1952.

"Bow of Pendleton Yields Seaman's Body." *Cape Cod Standard-Times*, February 25, 1952.

"Heroes of 1952 Return to the Sea." *Cape Cod Times*, May 16, 2002.

"Lurid Stories Crop Up." *Cape Codder*, February 28, 1952.

"Plight of 40 Fathoms Last Week Overlooked for Tanker Wrecks." *Cape Codder*, February 28, 1952.

"Salvage Work on Pendleton Watched." *Cape Codder*, August 16, 1956.

"Rescue Boat Rescue Underway." *Cape Codder*, November 17, 1981.

"Volunteers to the Rescue." *Cape Codder*, December 8, 1981.

"Coast Guardsmen Honored for Heroic Actions of Long Ago." *Cape Codder*, May 17, 2002.

"Sailors Rescued at Height of Storm." *Central Cape Press*, February 21, 1952.

"32 Rescued, 55 Cling to Split Ships Off Cape." *Daily Record*, February 19, 1952.

"Brant Point Crew Plows Through Seas." *Nantucket Town Crier*, February 22, 1952.

"Senate Unit Seeks Data on All Gains Made in Ship Deals." *The New York Times*, February 18, 1952.

"Snowstorm Kills 30 in New England." *The New York Times*, February 19, 1952.

"Two Ships Torn Apart." *The New York Times*, February 19, 1952.

"25 More Rescued in Tanker Wreck." *The New York Times*, February 20, 1952.

"Saw Tanker Peril." *The New York Times*, February 22, 1952.

"2 Tugs Tow Stern of Broken Tanker." *The New York Times*, February 22, 1952.

"57 Men Are Snatched from Sea." *Portland Herald Press*, February 19, 1952.

"Mercer Stern Safe." *Portland Herald Press*, February 22, 1952.

"Tanker Skipper." *Portland Herald Press*, February 22, 1952.

"15 Lost as 2 Tankers Split off Cape." *Standard-Times* (New Bedford, MA), February 19, 1952.

"Battered Ships, Weary Survivors Mark New Epic of Sea." *Standard-Times* (New Bedford, MA), February 20, 1952.

BOOKS AND MAGAZINE ARTICLES

Barbo, Theresa Mitchell, John Galluzzo, and Captain W. Russell Webster, USCG (Ret.). *The Pendleton Disaster Off Cape Cod: The Greatest Small Boat Rescue in Coast Guard History, a True Story.* Charleston, SC: History Press, 2010.

Dalton, J. W. *The Life Savers of Cape Cod.* Chatham, MA: Chatham Press, 1967 (reprint of 1902 edition).

Earle, W. K. "A Saga of Ships, Men and the Sea: When Two Ships Foundered Off Cape Cod, the Coast Guard Was Ready." *U.S. Coast Guard Magazine*, June 1952.

Farson, Robert H. *Twelve Men Down: Massachusetts Sea Rescues.* Orleans, MA: Cape Cod Historical Publications, 2000.

Frump, Robert. *Until the Sea Shall Free Them: Life, Death, and Survival in the Merchant Marine.* New York: Doubleday, 2001.

Fuller, Timothy, and Harry Friedenburg. "The Coast Guard's Finest Hour: The Day the *Pendleton* and the *Fort Mercer* Broke in Two." *Collier's Magazine*, December 27, 1952.

Hathaway, Charles B. *From Highland to Hammerhead: The Coast Guard and Cape Cod.* Self-published, 2000.

Johnson, Robert Erwin. *Guardians of the Sea: History of the United States Coast Guard, 1915 to the Present.* Annapolis, MD: U.S. Naval Institute Press, 1989.

Kaplan, H. R. *Voyager Beware.* Chicago, IL: Rand McNally, 1966.

Morris, Sid. "Ignore Blizzard—Return to Ship" (reprint of 1965 article). Available at http://www.sitnews.net/Acushnet/022403_SidMorris.html.

Noble, Dennis. *Rescued by the U.S. Coast Guard: Great Acts of Heroism Since 1878*. Annapolis, MD: U.S. Naval Institute Press, 2004.

Orleans Historical Society. *Rescue CG 36500*. Orleans, MA: Lower Cape Publishing, 1985.

Quinn, William P. *Shipwrecks Around Cape Cod*. Orleans, MA: Lower Cape Publishing, 1973.

————. *Shipwrecks Around New England*. Orleans, MA: Lower Cape Publishing, 1979.

Stancliff, Sherry S. "Fort Mercer and Pendleton Rescues." *Golden Tide Rips*, Class of 1950 Edition, 2000.

Tougias, Michael J., and Casey Sherman. *The Finest Hours: The True Story of the U.S. Coast Guard's Most Daring Sea Rescue*. New York: Scribner, 2009.

Webber, Bernard C. *Chatham: "The Lifeboatmen."* Orleans, MA: Lower Cape Publishing, 1985.

Webster, W. Russell. "The Pendleton Rescue." Available at http://www.cg36500.org/history_pendleton_rescue.html.

TURN THE PAGE FOR

THE **FINEST HOURS**

BONUS MATERIALS

An Interview with the Authors of *The Finest Hours*,

MICHAEL J. TOUGIAS AND CASEY SHERMAN

This book is an adaptation for young readers of an adult novel by the same title. What are some of the important changes you've implemented to make the story accessible to a younger audience?

MT: Very few changes were made to the action part of the book, but the more technical parts of the book were trimmed down (e.g., information about the building of the oil tanker). We also reduced the number of characters profiled. In retrospect, maybe we should have reduced the number of characters in the adult version too! If you focus on just a few characters, the reader can get to know them better and feel as if they actually met them.

What is the most fascinating thing you learned while doing research for *The Finest Hours*?

MT: In regard to the *Fort Mercer*, I was amazed how a single decision and some luck can mean the difference between life and death. For example, the *Fort Mercer* bow section sank just minutes after the last two men jumped overboard into the Coast Guard life raft. Had they hesitated, they would have gone down with the ship. On the other hand, the men on the stern section who decided to stay with the ship all survived in fine shape. The stern never sank despite all that damage!

CS: I learned about the challenges faced by the Coast Guard each and every day. We all seek safe harbor when bad weather hits, but the coasties have to go out into towering waves, hurricane winds, and sometimes blinding snow to save those who cannot save themselves.

Walt Disney Pictures is poised to release *The Finest Hours* movie. What do you think a new media will contribute to this wrenching story?

CS: The movie will be released in forty-six countries around the world, and we're excited for the opportunity to share this incredible story with those who may not speak our language or know anything about the coastline of Cape Cod. The theme of the story is universal for all audiences. It's a story about teamwork and faith—whatever your faith is.

What did you want to be when you grew up?

MT: I wanted to do something related to the outdoors, like be a forest ranger. I never really thought of becoming a writer, but there were clues going back to my childhood. I read every book I could get my hands on and especially enjoyed true adventure stories. I also kept a journal about my own adventures, so in a way I've been writing since I was nine years old.

CS: I wanted to be a tap dancer. Gene Kelly was my hero.

When did you realize you wanted to be a writer?

MT: When I was twenty-seven, my brother had a story published in a newspaper. I thought that was pretty cool, so I wrote a story for a magazine. When the magazine with my story arrived in my mailbox, I was so happy I began to write more stories for that magazine. Later I thought: Why not take the next step and write a book?

What's your most embarrassing childhood memory?

MT: I always thought I was this great outdoorsman and explorer. When our family and friends were vacationing on a lake, I announced I was going to paddle a canoe five miles around the lake on my own. I was about twelve years old and set out to conquer the lake, but it conquered me. A wind came up and kept slamming my canoe into the rocks on the far side of the lake, and I tried for an hour to get out of that jam. I was almost in tears when a man in a powerboat saw my predicament. He towed me back to my family. The worst part of the experience was that my entire family and all their friends were waiting on the dock, wondering who was in the canoe being towed. When a family friend realized it was me, he boomed out sarcastically, "Here comes Mike the Great!"

CS: When I almost fell off the stage during a tap dancing recital.

What's your favorite childhood memory?

MT: I spent all my free time exploring the woods and swamps near my home, and loved every minute. There was all kinds of wildlife and good fishing in the area. It made me want to buy a cabin in the woods. And later, when I graduated college, I did just that. My cabin eventually became the topic of *There's a Porcupine in My Outhouse!*, a book about all the weird experiences and misadventures that happened to me in the first year of owning the cabin and trying to live in the woods.

CS: Times spent with my father, who died when I was younger.

What was your favorite thing about school?

MT: Girls. I loved to make the girls laugh. And that got me in trouble. My favorite subject in school was history.

As a young person, who did you look up to most?

CS: My mother, who raised me, taught me right from wrong, and gave me the courage and drive to challenge myself to be the best I can be.

What were your hobbies as a kid? What are your hobbies now?

CS: I loved to read about exotic places as a kid, and now I get to travel to many of them as an adult.

Did you play sports as a kid?

CS: Yes, football and karate. Each taught me the value of discipline and teamwork.

MT: I was on the soccer team and was the worst player. I was also on the wrestling team and did really well, but I quit because there was too much pressure and the coach didn't know how to make the practices fun. I most enjoyed playing football in pickup games, but I was too small to make the high school team.

What was your first job, and what was your "worst" job?

MT: First job was cutting people's lawns. Later I worked in my father's bakery—that was tough because you had to get up at four a.m. to bake the bread. But I held jobs from supermarket stock boy to custodian. And I saved almost every penny to buy my cabin.

What book is on your nightstand now?

MT: I'm reading Maya Angelou's *I Know Why the Caged Bird Sings*. She is a great writer.

Where do you write your books?

MT: One of my most productive spots is on the screen porch at my cabin in Vermont. There are no Internet or cell phone connections there. And when I'm tired of writing, I can walk down to the lake and take a swim.

CS: I write in my little office, surrounded by books and research materials. My little dog, Maisy, sleeps at my feet.

What was your favorite book when you were a kid? Do you have a favorite book now?

MT: I read one book every two weeks, so I've read thousands. Three books that stand out are *The Killer Angels* by Michael Shaara, *Seabiscuit* by Laura Hillenbrand, and *To Kill a Mockingbird* by Harper Lee.

If you could travel in time, where would you go and what would you do?

CS: I'd travel back to Paris in the 1920s to meet my literary heroes Ernest Hemingway and F. Scott Fitzgerald at Sylvia Beach's legendary book shop Shakespeare and Company.

What's the best advice you have ever received about writing?

MT: I never got any advice and never took a journalism course. The best thing for writers to do is follow their own instincts on how to write and what to write about.

What advice do you wish someone had given you when you were younger?

MT: Don't follow the crowd. Do what you want to do, not what your friends are doing. Do the things that bring you joy. Learn to say no. So many people get asked to do things, and they automatically say yes.

What would you do if you ever stopped writing?

CS: I would learn an instrument or paint. I need to be creative.

What do you want readers to remember about your books?

MT: That I was a versatile writer who could do rescue books but also humor books (*There's a Porcupine in My Outhouse* and *The Cringe Chronicles*) and a serious book about two teenagers with cancer, called *Derek's Gift*. That book is a true story.

If you were a superhero, what would your superpower be?

MT: X-ray vision—then I could see all the fish I'm not catching!

Do you have any strange or funny habits? Did you when you were a kid?

CS: To build my vocabulary, I would look at a word and try to create as many words from the letters as I could. I still do that today.

What do you consider to be your greatest accomplishment?

CS: Being a dad to two beautiful young ladies.

MT: First is raising two wonderful children. They are now in their twenties, and they're my best friends. Second is that while I was working full-time at a corporation, I devoted nights to writing my first novel, *Until I Have No Country*. I felt so passionate about that project because it is about the Native Americans during the first Indian War in America. I'm so glad I made that story come to life.

What would your readers be most surprised to learn about you?

CS: That my older brother and I were born on the same day four years apart.

A forty-seven-foot sailboat disappears during a calamitous storm, leaving behind three survivors in a life raft. As eighty-foot waves crash around the raft, four coast guardsmen brave the storm to rescue the survivors. But will they make it in time?

A STORM
TOO SOON

Keep reading for a sneak peek of this riveting true account of a rescue at sea.

THE WAVE

On board the *Sean Seamour II*, the men are recovering from the shock of capsizing. After activating the Global Position Indicating Radio Beacon (GPIRB), JP begins to assess the conditions inside the boat. He checks the portholes, then looks at the mast, where it comes down through the deck to rest on the keel support grid. Both are in good shape. There is some water in the bilge, the lowest section inside the boat, below the floorboards. JP is able to quickly pump it out.

JP asks Ben and Rudy to sit on the floor on the starboard side of the vessel. The waves are beating against the port side, and he takes this precautionary measure so that no one is hurled from port to starboard if another rogue wave bears down on the boat. Checking the instruments, JP sees that the winds are out of the northeast, and he shudders to think what might have happened to the vessel if they were directly inside the Gulf Stream. The wind and waves are moving the boat at a steady clip of six knots toward the south-southwest. Though the Gulf Stream is to their west, JP calculates that they are well removed from it. They are, however, in a massive eddy of water warmed by the Gulf Stream, and there is nothing they can do about it. This eddy has moving currents that can increase the size of the waves.

The men have done all they can, so they sit quietly, waiting out the storm. No one can sleep with the wild motion of the boat and the ominous bangs on the hull from breaking waves. As the minutes go by, each man is lost in his own thoughts. JP assumes that the Coast Guard is working with the Automated Mutual-assistance Vessel Rescue System (Amver) to come to the *Sean Seamour II*'s rescue.

As the time approaches three a.m., JP makes a rudder adjustment. He wants to keep the port side slightly more exposed to the waves than the stern for better stability in sync with the drogue, which was fed off the stern. The boat does not respond as he expects it to, and he is puzzled by the loss of control. After lurching to a porthole in the galley, he can see that the drogue line is taut and assumes it is still attached, but he wonders about the lack of control. He also wonders why the Coast Guard has not called on the satellite phone. He moves to the chart table, takes a seat, and decides to call the Coast Guard, hoping there is a satellite in reception range.

Before he has time to make the call, the boat starts to roll.

It passes the 45-degree mark, and the men hold their breath as their eyes widen in fear and disbelief. For a brief, agonizing second, time seems to stop. They feel that they are carried by some unearthly force as the boat continues to turn beyond the 90-degree mark and their world goes upside down. It's a surreal, sickening feeling, even worse than the first knockdown, because this is happening more slowly, giving them time to realize the pure horror of it all. The lights flicker, and a low rumble gains volume as it comes from beyond the confines of the cabin. The rolling motion accelerates and seemingly defies gravity as objects are hurled from one side of the vessel to the other, crashing upon impact. Rudy and Ben are awkwardly pitched into a tumble as the *Sean Seamour II* does a complete 180-degree roll, caught inside the vortex of the wave. JP also starts to fall but is simultaneously slammed by the heavy salon table that has come free of its legs.

Buckets of green seawater flood into the upside-down sailboat.

The vessel has been struck by a colossal rogue wave that marine experts will later estimate is a minimum of eighty feet tall. It is possible that two waves joined forces to create one mass of energy. However it formed, there is no question about its power as it swallows the *Sean Seamour II*, whose mast is now pointing toward the bottom of the ocean.

JP struggles to breathe. Although his head is above the rising water, he's in excruciating pain and suspects he has broken ribs from the impact of the table. Then he feels the water climb up the back side of his neck and head, followed by silence as his ears submerge. He frantically fights to free himself, but he's pinned by the tabletop. *I'm going to drown inside my own boat!* Every neuron and nerve in his body is firing, and adrenaline courses through his limbs, but he cannot move.

Rudy is prone on the ceiling, which has become the floor of the capsized vessel. It takes him a couple of seconds to process what has happened. A single wall lamp is still on, and the first thing he sees is water shooting through two air vents as if someone is outside with a fire hose. Then he hears shouts: "Help! Help!" He looks toward the cries and, in the dim light, can see a mess of debris, including the tabletop. The top half of JP's head is barely visible above water.

Ben is also disoriented, but JP's hollering snaps him back to reality, and he heads toward the shouting. With Rudy, he pushes the table off JP and pulls the captain's head and shoulders out of the water. JP winces and groans as sharp pain spreads through his chest; slowly, he gets to his feet.

Almost two feet of water is sloshing about, with more gushing up through the ceiling vents below them. Aside from the incoming water, all is quiet. A couple of minutes go by as each man gathers himself and begins to process what has occurred. Ben is waiting for the vessel to right itself, but nothing happens. One thought races through his mind: *I don't want to die trapped inside. Rather die topside. See the sky one last time.* Rudy is having the same thought, and he stumbles to where the sliding companionway hatch should be. He takes off his personal flotation device (PFD), which hydrostatically inflated, but JP steps toward him, grabs him by the shoulders, and croaks, "Stay here!"

JP manages to ignore the throbbing in his chest. He has one thing on his mind: the life raft. *Is it still with the boat? If the boat doesn't right itself, we're going to need it.* He looks down where the companionway should be and takes a big breath of air. Searing pain shoots through his ribs. Then he lowers himself into the three feet of water and disappears.

Ben and Rudy stare down at the spot where JP submerged himself. A minute goes by and he does not surface. Water sloshes from one side of the vessel to the other, carrying all manner of debris. Rudy kneels down in the water. He sticks his head under and starts to pull his body toward where he believes the companionway hatch should be. He can't see a thing, and he gropes around, trying to feel for either JP or the hatch. He's running out of air and comes back to the surface. He shakes his head at Ben, indicating the futility of his dive. The two men look each other directly in the eye. It is their absolute lowest moment. *Did JP get stuck? Is he drowned? Did the waves take him away?* A creeping panic rises between them, spawned by the feeling that they are entombed. And the water is rising.

∼

JP somehow manages to slide open the hatch and swim out, barely able to hold his breath. He needs air, yet he doesn't shoot directly for the surface. Instead, he lets his hands feel their way to the starboard leg of the arch that rises from the stern of the boat, not far from the companionway hatch. He sweeps with his arm, feeling for the life raft canister, and follows the arch to the port side. Still no raft. It should be in the canister just a few inches aft of the arch. His lungs are screaming for air, and he's fighting their call. He can sense that his body will ignore the commands from his brain to hold his breath and that his mouth will open on its own.

Grabbing hold of the toe rail, JP plans to pull himself toward the surface by following the upside-down hull. Suddenly, the boat starts to right itself. It all happens so fast that there is no time to think, and JP holds on as best he can. Incredibly, he lands in a heap in the cockpit next to the helm as the boat rolls out of its capsized position.

Coughing, gagging, and desperately sucking in big gulps of air, the captain is exhausted and disoriented. Five or six seconds go by before he notices a dim light coming from an opening, and he realizes that he's in the cockpit, looking down the companionway steps. The light is coming from the cabin. Hope! The *Sean Seamour II* has something left in her; she's not done yet. A new shot of adrenaline courses through his body, temporarily blocking out the pain of the broken ribs.

Then he remembers that the raft is gone, and his spirits plunge as quickly as they rose. He glances under the arch at an empty space where the raft and canister were mounted on the boat. *Without the raft, we are as good as dead. The boat is on borrowed time.*

The battered captain steals another look down the companionway and realizes the top part of the companionway hatch is gone.

He shouts down to Ben and Rudy, "Get the pumps running! I've got to find the raft!"

As JP's eyes adjust to the darkness, he takes a second to collect himself, kneeling in the pulpit area of the cockpit, which is just forward of the wheel. The *Sean Seamour II* is a bit more stable in the raging seas now that it is filled with thousands of pounds of water.

A wave slides beneath the vessel, and when the boat is in the bottom of the canyon, it is eerily quiet, almost serene, giving JP the feeling that he and his crew are the last humans alive on the planet. Then the next wave carries the vessel up to the wind-whipped summit, where his senses are blasted by the roar of breaking seas. With a smudge of moonlight filtering through the cloud cover, he can see the outlines of the mountainous waves and the white water at their crests. The sight is so incredible, so unlike anything he's ever seen, that he has to force himself to look away and focus on the boat. That's when he notices that the mast has been cracked, just above deck level, off its base. It is lying off to the port side of the boat, almost parallel to the hull. The lower half of the mast is resting on top of the vessel, and its upper half is in the water. The rigging is a complete mess.

JP squints at the water beneath where the mast is lying. *The raft!* He can't believe it. The raft is fully inflated and pinned against the water by a spreader that extends from the mainmast at a right angle. That the raft wasn't snatched away by the waves borders on the miraculous. But to be able to use the raft, JP will have to remove it from beneath the spreader.

The captain is so determined that for now he is keeping fear at bay. He doesn't stop to think about the fact that he is not tethered to the *Sean Seamour II* and could be thrown off at any second. He inches toward the raft, which appears to be upside down. The ballast bags that normally hang beneath the raft and fill with water for stabilization are on the top, and one of them looks to be pierced by the spreader.

JP has a high tolerance for pain, having experienced severe burns in childhood, but now the adrenaline rush is wearing off, and every movement of the boat causes agony that can't be ignored.

He knows the pain will soon become debilitating. In order to survive, JP must free the raft immediately.